ELSINORE

The *City of Hate* Conspiracy

Terry Michaels
with
Blair Woodcock

Dedicated to Carly Skelton:
my sunshine when skies are grey.

Elsinore: The *City of Hate* Conspiracy
Copyright © 2016 Terry Michaels
First edition, 2016
Printed in the
United States of America
Edited by Blair Woodcock
***

Cover design by Steven McAdam
www.linkedin.com/in/smcadam

CONTENTS

Introduction

Television programs in the 1950s provide the impression that this period was an age of innocence in America. With *Ozzie and Harriet*, *Leave It To Beaver*, and countless other TV series promoting Judeo-Christian values, it's difficult to think otherwise. The *Roy Rogers Show* took a particularly bold stand for righteousness, to the point of inserting scripture in most episodes. Even now, I can hear in my mind Dale Evans Rogers quoting, "For all have sinned and fall short of the glory of God" (Romans 3:23). I would never have known such truths had it not been for that dear saint. Nor would I have known the "Happy Trails" that such wisdom can lead to.

Although God, country and family sat high in the saddle in the 1950s, the decade certainly had its low points. Somehow "equal rights" and "equal opportunity" didn't always make the cut as traditionally accepted values. Not yet. Women weren't as privileged as men, nor were blacks as privileged as whites.

So-called "God-fearing patriots" showed further contempt for the Jewish community. These sentiments carried over from the 1940s when Jews were wrongfully blamed for initiating wars for profit, dominating the banking business, and jeopardizing the economy. Surprisingly, industrialist Henry Ford during that time became one of the most influential voices spewing this sort of poison.

Ford's influence lost its punch after the Holocaust of World War II. The senseless slaughter of countless innocents drew great sympathy for the Jewish people. The alternative to sympathizing was to be labeled a Nazi, and few citizens wanted that. Yet at the same time, there was little rejoicing when Jews laid hold of the American Dream. Few Americans wanted that either. For this reason, many Americans resented their Jewish neighbors.

Bigotry wasn't the sole of society's ills. There was also the Cold War. Communist dictators had spread great terror into many parts of the world. Those persecuted under communist regimes compared what they suffered to the Jewish suffering under the Nazis. In those lands, prison and torture awaited anyone unwilling to conform to communist doctrine and rule. The threat of communism advancing into America, the Land of the Free, created widespread panic and paranoia.

Government watchdog groups were tasked to investigate any suspicious activity on the home front. On the federal level there was the House UnAmerican Activities Committee (HUAC). HUAC was initially formed to uncover and expose citizens who had potential ties to the Nazis. In the 1950s, the focus shifted to communist infiltrators. This was largely due to the influence of Joseph McCarthy, whose name is often synonymous with witch-hunting. Though communism was a genuine threat in his day, the broad brush of McCarthyism deemed many Americans guilty by association.

Watchdog organizations also existed at the state level. In the Golden State, the California Senate Factfinding Subcommittee on UnAmerican Activities (SUAC) monitored anyone showing shades of communistic red. And when a few red spots appeared in a sleepy, small, southern California town, all eyes suddenly converged on Elsinore.

Communism wasn't Elsinore's only threat. Local residents were worried about their water supply. Many feared losing their water completely, resulting in an evaporation of tourism dollars. Others were convinced that the water was turning toxic, largely due to its high fluoride content, even though little was known about fluoride in the 1950s. In those days it was mainly government agencies that warned of fluoride's potential dangers. Not all were convinced, however, and resident communists in Elsinore alleged that the "fluoride hoax" was just a scare tactic used by an evil government to run off the growing Jewish population.

During this turbulent time, my father Pat Michaels worked as a reporter with KTLA television station in Los Angeles. He not only covered the Elsinore story, but he also created and aired a controversial television documentary about the events swirling around the city. The one-hour TV program was called *City of Hate*. Pat's was not the only report. SUAC investigators had their own version of the story.

The account in *Elsinore* is historical fiction based on SUAC findings, my father's broadcasts, court records, and newspaper articles. *Elsinore* is the story of a small resort with enormous personalities and monster fears. *Elsinore* is the story that history tried to bury. The events are true, but the dialogue (unless otherwise noted) springs from creative license. When information was lacking, I added development to the characters and recreated scenes.

The National Jewish POST and OPINION
Friday, December 25, 1959

"Officials Hit TV Broadcast Saying Jews In Calif. Town Terrorized"

LOS ANGELES (P-O) — The Pacific Southwest Regional Office of ADL (Anti-Defamation League) this week blasted as "hysteria" an hour-long telecast describing a condition of "terror" for Jews living in the resort town of Elsinore, halfway between Los Angeles and San Diego. The station KTLA telecast by Pat Michaels, "City of Hate," touched off a wave of fear and apprehension within the Southern California Jewish community. In a report to Southland B'nai B'rith presidents, Regional ADL director Milton A. Senn charged that the telecast was "compounded of fact, fiction, speculation and hysteria," according to *Heritage*, Anglo-Jewish weekly published by Herb Brin. Senn said that for a year and a half the ADL has been investigating reports of anti-Semitic incidents that formed the surface of a political squabble over water rights. Last year *Heritage* broke the Elsinore story exclusively, winning third prize for a news story in California Newspaper Publishers Association competition.

Heritage reported last week that "Michaels took a serious issue and a series of events stretching over a period of a year and a half in time—and compressed it all into an often frightening report, out of context, as though it were all

11

happening now rather than over a protracted period of time." "Charges that the Jews of Elsinore are terrorized, live in fear and trepidation, and that the city itself seethes with anti-Jewish hostility which 'parallels the nightmare of Nazi Germany with frightening fidelity' is sheer hysteria," Senn said.

The ADL director said, "charges that there is a conspiracy to drive the Jews out of Elsinore, that the fight over mineral water is motivated by this Judenrein wish, or that the State Department of Health is a witting tool in this conspiracy—all this is pure speculation or suspicion." Senn said, "Anti-Semitic activity in Elsinore, it is agreed by all knowledgeable persons, including Mr. Michaels, is the handiwork of a few people." There have been incidents of vandalism, anonymous letters and crackpot pamphlets. These are facts," he said.

"But," Senn added, "Mr. Michaels asserted that the Jews of Elsinore—who number about 400 out of a total population of 2,300 —were given six months to get out of Elsinore or there would be bloodshed. This is fiction. At another point Mr. Michaels said that the Jews of Elsinore were given six months to get out of the city or be killed. This, too, is fiction." Senn said the telecast was made without the knowledge of the ADL, although the station learned, in the course of preparing its material, of the league's deep involvement in the problem.

"We learned of the telecast for the first time when KTLA's publicity department asked us to help publicize it in the

Jewish community. We refused to do so without knowing the program's content. Subsequently, KTLA held a press preview to which we were not invited," Senn said. Eventually Senn and Joseph Roos of the Jewish Federation - Council's Community Relations Committee arranged with KTLA's general manager for a preview. Senn urged the manager and Michaels to change the name of the show "on the grounds that it was an unfortunate and sensational title which was not justified either by the content of the show or the facts." I also pointed out that "some of the editorial comment exaggerated the facts and drew unwarranted conclusions," Senn said, but he was told that "some material would be added at the beginning and the end of the show to beef it up but that the title would not be changed, mainly because of its dramatic impact."

The Desert Sun, Palm Springs CA
Number 136, 6 January 1961

"Grand Jury Acts in Elsinore Case Riverside"

Twelve indictments were handed down yesterday by the Riverside County Grand Jury as a result of preliminary investigations into Elsinore's controversy - wracked "City of Hate" telecast on a Los Angeles TV channel in 1959. And, the Grand Jury indicated, the investigation is still continuing.

Indicted by the jurors on charges of conspiracy to commit slander were: Pat Michaels, onetime commentator for Station KTLA Channel 5, which aired the "City of Hate" broadcast; Police Chief Walter Bittle, Mayor Thomas Bartlett, realtor Sam Farber, retired businessman Ben Kagan, City Attorney Carl S. Kegley, retired optical wholesaler Morris Kominsky and former KTLA executive James Schulke. City Attorney Kegley was also indicted for presenting false claims to the City of Elsinore for telephone bills during January and June of 1950

The entire Elsinore City Council - Mayor Bartlett and councilmen Thomas Yarborough. Joseph Davidson, Roy Macy and Richard McAdams - was indicted for conspiracy to violate terms of a water permit issued by the State Department of Public Health in its Sept, 8 action ordering 100 per cent mineral water into the city's general water supply.

14

Still under investigation by the Grand Jury is alleged subversive activity directed against both Gentile and Jewish people, improper voter registration procedures, violations of the Brown (anti-secrecy) Act and "several evidences of perjured testimony before the Grand Jury. The conspiracy charges brought against the group are punishable by up to three years imprisonment. Criminal complaints, issuable by the Riverside County District Attorney, are needed to proceed in the indictment situation.

1

Shattered

January 1958

It certainly wasn't the most romantic movie, especially for a first date, but it was the only show in town. John Kneubuhl's debut horror film, The Screaming Skull, had finally made it to the big screen in Elsinore, promising enough chills to give Godzilla goose bumps. Sadly, the low budget creep-show failed to deliver, at least for two fearless teens. Instead, Ralph and Eunice strolled out of Lake Theatre giggling like junior-high kids undressing in a locker room for the first time.

"Mom says Kneubuhl writes TV westerns," Eunice remarked. "He needs to stick with cowboys and forget haunted heads, if you ask me."

"C'mon, it wasn't that bad." Ralph objected.

"The whole idea was preposterous."

"Preposterous!" Ralph teased. "You're preposterous!"

"Now, that's no way to treat a lady."

"How bout I treat you to ice cream then."

"I don't know, Ralph. It's getting late."

"That movie didn't frighten you, but you're afraid of the dark?"

"I'm not afraid of the dark." Eunice explained. "I'm afraid of thugs."

"Thugs in this sleepy town?"

"You did hear about those two gals that were kidnapped recently, didn't you?"

"That was a purse snatching, not a kidnapping."

"According to Kominsky they were abducted!"

"Morris Kominsky!" Ralph chuckled. "According to him the sky is falling. He's nothing but a crazy old Jew."

The racial slur went off like a Molotov cocktail in Eunice's head, leaving her with a disturbing ring in her ears. Stuck somewhere between fight and flight, she froze. Ralph turned to look at her, not knowing what to make of her silence. He was clueless as an eight ball. When her tears came, Ralph hoped an answer would float up out of nowhere, but that never happened.

Eventually an apology somehow surfaced from Ralph, but his attempt to square things fell flat. In the spirit his words were offered, Ralph wouldn't have stood a chance, even on bended knee. There was no contrition in his voice. Even his eyes betrayed him. He looked as if his Jewish insult was justified.

When Eunice didn't respond, Ralph scoffed, "Didn't know you had such a soft spot for Kominsky."

"I suppose you think I'm as crazy as he is." Eunice blubbered.

"Now, why would I think that?"

"Me being a Jew and all."

"You're Jewish?" Ralph gasped with visible shock.

"Sorry to disappoint you."

Ralph's shocked reaction was the last straw for Eunice. She dashed off in an angry huff, ignoring Ralph's desperate pleas.

"I'm sorry!" he cried repeatedly, but Eunice wasn't in a forgiving mood. Her only interest was finding someplace where she could be alone, somewhere safe.

By the time Ralph caught up with her, Eunice was sitting in front of the local synagogue, staring at the stained glass window above. Cautiously, he approached her from behind. It was apparent that she was still crying. Ralph never meant to cause such heartbreak. He felt terrible. Finally.

Why did it matter that she was Jewish? Ralph reasoned as if a light came on for the first time in his mind. After he reached out and tentatively took her hand, only love mattered. As for Eunice, it was the Hebrew inscription above her that mattered to her most. Etched in stained glass were words written long ago - The Ten Commandments.

After a long silence, Eunice spoke. "Are you a religious person, Ralph?"

"I believe in God, if that's what you mean."

"So you also believe in the Shalts and Shalt Nots?" Eunice pointed up at the twin tablets in the glass.

"Without question."

"So, you agree we serve the same God?"

"Yeah, sure. I mean..." Ralph hesitated. "Well, you know, I'm a Methodist. We believe in Jesus and all that."

"Oh, of course, Jesus!" Eunice grinned. "He's a Jew, right?"

This time the explosion went off in Ralph's head. He got the point.

Eunice finally accepted his apology. Their reconciliation was sealed with a tender embrace. Ralph wanted to linger in her arms forever, and neither noticed as they snuggled that one of the local high-school jocks and his two sidekicks happened to walk up on the sidewalk behind them. The confidence levels of the bully Daniel and his buddies were higher than their combined IQ's. All brawn. Little need for brain. It soon became obvious that they were strolling through Elsinore looking for trouble.

"Now ain't that cute." Daniel the ringleader heckled. "Will you look at those two lovebirds!"

"Take a hike." Eunice shot back.

"Oh, you got a feisty one there, Ralph," Laughed Daniel. "She bringing you to temple to get circumcised?"

"Mind your business." Eunice scolded loudly.

"The rabbi ain't in, Ralphy." Daniel mocked. "Maybe we can help. I have my trusty pocketknife with me. Sharpened it this morning just for the occasion."

Ralph spoke up. "I'll tell you where to stick that knife." He sputtered loudly.

"Come here and tell me to my face if you got the guts."

Ralph's adrenaline was pumping and his honor was in question. He wasn't in his right mind. No one could have reasoned with him when he charged down the steps to attack his adversaries. He didn't stand a Popsicle's chance in a potter's kiln, however. Within minutes Ralph's bruised and bloodied body lay limp in a bed of gravel. Daniel did a victory dance while Eunice sobbed uncontrollably beneath the "Big Ten."

"I did you a favor, girl," Daniel boasted. "Matter of fact, you owe me a big kiss for clobbering that weasel."

Daniel boldly marched toward Eunice, lips puckering. With every step he was threatening to claim his prize. As Eunice shrunk back in terror, Ralph raised his head. He mustered barely enough strength to pull himself to his feet. By the curb Ralph noticed a baseball-sized rock, and he reached for it with his throwing hand. Still a bit groggy, he carefully took aim and hurled the projectile at Daniel. All five of them watched that night as the rock sailed above Daniel's head, directly toward the synagogue's expensive, historic, and revered stained glass window. They heard the loud crash. All eyes widened as they stared at the large hole atop the Sixth Commandment.

Then they heard a loud, shrill voice coming from down the street, shouting out from the front door of Lucky's Diner. "I'm calling the cops."

Like scared rats on a sinking ship, Daniel and his two cohorts fled the scene into the night. Ralph, still dizzy from getting the stuffing pounced out of him, didn't know what to do. Eunice insisted he head home while she waited for the police. She'd take care of things. She'd concoct a story. The kind of story that Morris Kominsky, local communist agitator, was known to tell.

2

The Crescent

On any given day, Morris Kominsky could be found in the center of town, seated on one of several rockers on the porch in front of the huge old Chimes building on Graham Street. Morris was a striking man, who may have passed as Humphrey Bogart if not for the crow's feet drooping down from his eyes and trailing the length of his middle-aged face. Years of worry had engraved those lines there, and there were trenches of equal depth on his furrowed brow.

Some people thought Morris had too much time on his hands, puffing away on his pipe for hours and buttonholing anyone who happened to stroll by, talking to them incessantly. Townspeople in a hurry opted to walk on the opposite side of the road. Despite the garrulous reputation that prompted some to avoid him, Morris never ran short of company. Everyone in town agreed that he was the main source for local news. Known for tall tales, Morris especially loved to boast of his chance encounter in the late 1940s with actor Steve McQueen.

"I was sitting in this very chair," he swore. "There was a loud rumbling and roaring. Before I could blink, he shows up out of nowhere on a motorcycle.

"I was a bit aggravated, honestly," Morris would tell his listeners. "And I didn't even recognize this budding film star McQueen. I started chastising him for disturbing my peace. His big motorcycle kicked up a huge dust storm less than a yard in front of my face!

"We don't need trouble around here, I scolded the lad. But young Steve didn't want trouble either. He just wanted to take a bath! I had to laugh. He came two years too late, because the bathhouses in The Chimes were already closed by then!"

There was a time when The Chimes building hosted a steady stream of visitors. It was the most impressive bathhouse within hundreds of miles. Built in 1887 by Elsinore's founder Franklin Heald, the Victorian-style structure designed by Frank Ferris boasted of Roman tubs, steam rooms, and hot mud baths.

Morris would continue telling the story. "I informed McQueen that this place was called The Crescent back in the old days. Folks came from all over to unwind here. Important people like Clark Gable and that fella' from the Tarzan movies, Johnny Weissmuller."

Morris would tell his listeners that the young McQueen already knew a lot of these important movie stars. And McQueen also had read all about The Crescent and the long list of celebrities who had visited there. That's what had brought him to Elsinore in the first place—Steve wanted to see the place for himself. Not only that, but he had also heard of those healing waters, and he believed they were crying out for him to experience them.

"I finally broke the bad news to the poor chap," Morris would recall. "After water levels dropped in Elsinore's wells, business also evaporated. The Crescent soon shut its doors. It's now an antique store."

Morris said that McQueen was still curious enough to look inside, however. "Enter at your own risk!" Morris had warned the actor. "The place is haunted!"

Morris wasn't the only one in town to believe ghosts occupied the aging walls of The Chimes. Many such stories were well known, and they existed long before Morris had arrived in town. Rumors became especially rampant in 1939 after the son of Elsinore's Deputy Sheriff drowned in the courtyard swimming pool. People swore the boy's spirit never left.

Apparitions of another young girl, Gloria, had also been reported. An auto accident in front of The Crescent had claimed her mother's life along with the poor child's legs; both legs had to be amputated. Gloria was eventually brought to The Crescent for therapy. Sadly, the mineral water failed to prolong her life beyond childhood.

"I warned McQueen that he might hear Gloria crying for her mother," said Morris. "And there was once a teddy bear that someone had put in The Crescent in memory of Gloria, but at regular intervals the stuffed bear would change resting places... by itself... unexplained."

Morris would continue, "And I told Steve not to sit on either of those old motorcycles in there either, because spooks watched over those, too!"

According to Morris's description of that day's events, McQueen walked into The Crescent, but he bolted out within five minutes. "I could see the sweat dripping from his forehead. That's when I directed McQueen to another place where he could get a bath."

No one ever disagreed that The Crescent had opened wide the door of tourism to Elsinore. Even before this large edifice was built, however, the area's healthful waters were well known to earlier inhabitants of the land. The waters for decades had aroused the attention of the many curious seekers of the unusual. Native Americans, Spanish missionaries, and Mexican Ranchers all believed that health and happiness sprang from the magical wells. The fact that the settlement was situated on the bank of Southern California's largest natural lake was a helpful draw, too.

Nevertheless, it was the mineral springs that made Elsinore the esteemed resort city it was soon to become. In time, tourists arrived in droves, soaking in the springs as if they had tapped into a divine resource. Some imagined that the waters were from the Tree of Life itself.

With the railroad station immediately across the street, The Crescent couldn't keep pace with all the people arriving. It didn't take long for other businesses to sprout up, helping to accommodate Elsinore's numerous visitors. A host of inns, spas, and swimming holes soon transformed the dusty community into a recreational hot spot. Most of these businesses were Jewish owned, and before long Jews made up one third of the population—although not all of Elsinore's residents were pleased with this statistic.

Around this time a prolonged drought had turned much of Southern California, with the exception of Elsinore, into a land resembling the Gobi Desert. In response, a statewide master plan was developed to import water from the Colorado River, sending it to various areas. Unfortunately, the plan also included the replacement of Elsinore's spring water—and this was a move that would quickly dry up tourism. Business owners adamantly objected. Sadly, their concerns were not shared by the powerbrokers in Sacramento. Elected bureaucrats had other worries, and safety was a chief one. As long as well-water levels in Elsinore remained low, fluoride levels remained high and, according to the government, highly toxic.

3

Special Delivery

August 1956

"We mourn today the loss of one of Hollywood's greatest legends," Pat Michaels lamented during his evening radio broadcast. "Famous for his role as Count Dracula, actor Bela Lugosi has seen the last of vampires, and has been swept away by angels from above."

Lugosi was especially familiar to the people of Elsinore. The town was Bela's home away from home. Whereas most celebrities stayed at the local inn, Lugosi secured his own private quarters near the center of town.

He was a peculiar fellow, locals agreed. To quote Lugosi, as Pat did in his tribute, "Every actor is somewhat mad, or else he'd be a plumber or a bookkeeper or a salesman."

It was never easy for Pat to announce the loss of his beloved celebrities. Their fame and riches fascinated him, and it took all the self-control he had not to become choked up when one of them died. If by chance his emotions got the better of him during a broadcast, he blamed the cigarette smoke that continually clogged his lungs for choking him up. On this occasion, however, it was clear that the news of Lugosi's passing was the source of Pat's sorrow. His quivering lower lip was almost perceptible as he shared the news with his listeners.

Pat signed off the air that evening with his customary "Good night folks, and good news tomorrow."

The "on-air" light went out and Pat clicked off the microphone. He heard one of his producers calling him. "Pat! Phone call for you!"

Pat stood up and walked to his colleague. "Thanks, Jack," he said, taking the receiver. "Hello?" he said.

"This is Saint Joseph's Hospital," declared the nurse on the other end. "It's a boy! Eight pounds, six ounces. Perfectly healthy!"

Pat's eyes widened, and any remaining sorrow about Lugosi's death melted away into joy. He covered the mouthpiece with his hand. "A boy! It's a boy!" he shouted to the crew milling around the studio.

"Congrats!" several employees replied, smiling at him and saluting him cheerfully.

"This is great!" cried Pat into the phone. "Tell Lois I'll be right there!" He slammed down the phone and grabbed his hat. Minutes later his two-tone, red and white Buick was speeding down the freeway to the hospital in Orange, California. Pat couldn't wait to see what heaven had sent.

Pat Michaels had never planned to have children with his wife, but after the offspring started arriving he proudly welcomed them. Impetuosity and a careless disregard for minor details and plans were part of his nature in every aspect of life. He lived for the moment, oblivious to potential outcomes, letting the chips fall

28

where they may. The unknown didn't frighten him. He was a risk-taker, always treading close to the extreme edges of danger. Flirting with trouble was thrilling and fun.

And, in this case, if having fun meant another mouth to feed down the road, Pat's worldview told him there was no sense in worrying about it. It was the "here and now" that mattered most. Forget consequences.

Some thought that Pat's risk-taking behavior was reckless. Others considered him brave. The truth was, both evaluations were correct. Pat was recklessly brave, and these traits served him well as a reporter. In his journalistic mind, if a story wasn't worth going out on a limb for, it simply wasn't newsworthy. Never mind if the limb was just a bent and splintering green twig. Danger made the story grander.

Pat's daring approach to work and life was an asset in his reporting. But it was his greatest liability in his personal life.

"A boy, a boy…" Pat repeated as his four-door Riviera swerved through traffic. "Oh boy!"

If one more kid was to be added to the family, a boy was preferable. With two daughters and only one son so far, the latest arrival would even things out. Pat continued to rejoice as he mumbled, "Four kids. Swell! Two girls, two boys. Perfect."

Even with Pat's customary lack of forethought regarding the results of his actions, in one corner of his mind he realized that there was no need to have another baby after this one. The type of life he was leading was just too unpredictable. But the temptation to take risks would eventually prove stronger than Pat's common sense.

In 1956, the Michaels family was living together in a home nestled in the quiet suburbs of Santa Ana, California. Pat grew up in this town, and Santa Ana was where Pat met and married his high-school sweetheart, Lois. In their eyes, there was no better place to rear their children. Disneyland had just opened its doors nearby, making Orange County the happiest place on earth. The magical Disney aura seemed to permeate the local atmosphere and residents' attitudes. And the Michaels family was happy to live next to this new kingdom of tourists!

Always wanting to be in the center of the action, Pat drove his family to Disneyland on the day the park opened, motivated partly as family man, partly as reporter. Walt wasn't available for an interview, and Mickey Mouse was too busy passing out balloons, so Pat spent more time that day acting as a dad than as a reporter.

Although Santa Ana did hold a special place in Pat's heart, his vocational roots extended elsewhere. He quickly made a name for himself as the youngest war correspondent with the Mutual Broadcasting Company. Unfortunately, his coverage of the Korean War was cut short by a sniper, and he ended up in the hospital with a shoulder injury.

Shortly thereafter, Lois received word that Pat had died from his wound. This was a lie that Pat had concocted to cover up the fact that he had fallen irrationally in love with a nurse he met while recovering in an Australian military hospital. The love affair didn't last though. After

Pat discovered there was no future for him with the young Australian beauty, he was on the next plane leaving the continent.

Back in California, a chagrinned and contrite Pat Michaels climbed the stairs to his in-laws' doorstep, where his so-called "widow" and firstborn daughter were receiving shelter and care as they grieved about Pat's untimely demise.

When Lois saw Pat again, she almost fainted in shock and surprise. Many painful conversations followed during the next few days, as Pat awkwardly confessed his wrongdoings.

Against the objections of her father, Lois accepted Pat back into her life and home. Hers had turned now to a love based on affection, but certainly not based on trust. Pat's proclivity toward wandering eyes left little hope for trust.

With his fresh new start, Pat soon picked up where he left off in pursuing his dream as a journalist. His ambitions took him from city to city and from state to state—from New Orleans to San Antonio and to many other locations. There wasn't anywhere he wasn't willing to travel to build his career. Finally, after years of paying dues by working in faraway places, Pat was glad when he received a job offer from KWIZ Radio in Santa Ana. It was time to return to more familiar surroundings and bigger paychecks.

Pat often boasted that his journalistic genes were inherited. "My father lived for the newspaper business, until toxic printer's ink called him to a more peaceful existence six feet under!"

In truth, Pat never knew his father. Born in the mid-1920s to unprepared teenaged parents, it wasn't long before young Pat was placed into foster care. His formative years were spent in a Wisconsin orphanage run by strict Polish-speaking nuns with fists of steel. Fortunately, his mother married before he reached adolescence, and the newlyweds acted quickly to rescue the dejected and struggling youth from his grim and cold existence. The small family relocated to Santa Ana, where Pat could be raised in a better environment.

And now Pat was making news in the city where his dreams were first conceived, working at the town's most popular radio station, where all who knew him could hear his stellar voice. He felt he was about to hit the big-time.

If one had the radio antenna adjusted just right, one could even hear the voice of Pat Michaels in Elsinore.

Pat finally arrived at the hospital that day to meet his new son. The kid was great, but naming this fourth child became a matter of debate between Pat and his wife. Lois wanted the name "Cary" whereas Pat preferred "Terrance."

The name "Terrance" complemented the Irish identity that Pat had created for himself a few years earlier, right after fighting the Nazis in World War II. At that time, Pat began thinking about a name change for himself. He went through the entire legal process to have his German surname "Krone" exchanged for the more Gaelic-sounding "Michaels." This decision involved name changes for his wife and two daughters as well.

The newborn didn't require a name change. Like his older brother, the surname "Michaels" was handed to him on a birth certificate.

As for the baby's first name, Pat had his way with Lois again. His wife surrendered—and the boy's name became Terrance.

4
Fluoride Scare

Although she wasn't an environmental expert, Elsinore mayor Cheryl French left the city council meeting that day feeling confident that she had made a strong case against fluoride. She had served a drinking glass filled halfway with salt to each attendee. Cheryl then topped each glass with water.

"Bottoms up!" she chuckled as she took the first sip. One by one, the rest of the board members followed suit. As predicted, the closer their lips drew to the salt, the more intolerable the taste became.

"Cheryl, with all due respect," said one of town officials. "Have you lost your mind? We can't drink all this!"

"Right! Salt in small doses is fine," Cheryl asserted. "Our favorite recipes would be bland without a dash here or sprinkle there."

"If we drank this entire glass," Councilman Webber interjected, "we'd all end up in the hospital with salt poisoning."

"Exactly my point!" Cheryl exclaimed triumphantly. "Now think of that glass as a mineral spring, similar to those wonderful springs that serve our resort community so well. And think of all that salt as the fluoride resting at the bottom of each of our wells."

"You have our attention, Cheryl," Webber nodded. "Your conclusion is?"

"With well water levels as low as they are currently because of this interminable drought, we are consuming a higher ratio of fluoride than ever before. Small doses of fluoride may be fine, but after years of no rain, our wells have become fluoride tubs. Everyone in town is at risk."

"So says the State Department of Public Health," Webber snorted sarcastically.

"We're in no position to say otherwise," Cheryl intoned. "Even if one person falls ill from fluoride, I don't want that illness to be on me. Do you? And what if fluoride poisoning brings even worse consequences than sickness?"

Cheryl's question hung in the air as the board members looked at one another silently. After a few moments, Webber nodded slightly. Cheryl sensed victory and repressed a slight smile. She could see that the group was getting the point.

A few other sundry matters were discussed that day, and then the meeting was adjourned. Cheryl stood up, confident she had successfully united the council to comply with mandates from the state of California to restrict the Elsinore residents from using their water that contained such high levels of fluoride.

As it turned out, Cheryl's taste of victory lost its flavor the instant she stepped out of the town hall and onto the sidewalk. She saw him almost immediately. Morris Kominsky.

Oh no, she thought. Blathering away as usual in front of The Chimes. She also saw local rancher Slim Wiggins in his blue overalls, rocking on the chair next to Morris. Slim was a devotee and acolyte of Morris, and he hung on Morris's every word. Slim believed any rumors Morris spewed as if they were fact.

Mayor French was about to cross the street to avoid the pair, but the opportunity evaporated when Morris caught sight of her.

"Oh look!" cried Morris to Slim. "Speak of the devil! Why there's our esteemed Mayor French now!"

Cheryl felt the blood rush to her face as Morris continued. "I know you just came from a city council meeting!" he called to her. "And I know what you were talking about! You can't let this happen! You can't let the state dilute our mineral water and take away our tourist industry and our livelihoods! The mineral water is our bread and butter! It's like gold! It's what put Elsinore on the map!"

"It's out of my hands." Cheryl told Morris as she approached The Chimes.

"Baloney! You're the mayor!"

"A small-town mayor," Cheryl reminded him as she continued walking along the sidewalk. "I'm not Governor Knight, you know!"

"You have influence." Morris argued. "Stand up to those crooked state bureaucrats!"

Cheryl stopped and looked at Kominsky. "I've done all I can, Morris. The entire city council has tried, but we can't fight the power of the state."

Slim was leaning forward, listening intently. His lips formed a tight line and he wasn't buying this woman mayor's story. He believed in his heart that Kominsky was right and the mayor was lying. In anger, Slim suddenly jumped off his porch rocker and leaped down the three steps from the porch. He rushed to the sidewalk and confronted the mayor to her face.

"If we lose our water…" Slim sputtered, "You'll not only have the whole town to answer to, but you'll be out of a job! Or worse!" Slim jabbed his finger toward her face.

Cheryl drew back. "I will not be threatened," Cheryl said, although the wavering tone in her voice belied her words. Slim was not a large man, but he towered over the pint-sized Cheryl by more than a foot. Cheryl glanced over at Morris pleadingly. Morris rose from his chair.

Although they certainly had their differences, Morris still had enough chivalry in him to defend a woman that he perceived was in distress. "Slim! Slim! Simmer down!" he called. "There's no need for violence comrade!"

Morris descended the porch steps and walked toward the two rivals. "We're all concerned about the situation! No need to blow your stack Slim! Calm yourself! Truth will prevail. Don't you worry! I'll make sure of that!"

Morris positioned himself between Slim and Cheryl, and Slim turned away sharply in anger and spit into the dust by the road. Cheryl was visibly shaken.

Morris lowered his voice as he faced Cheryl. "Miss Mayor, we can't lose our water. You know that, don't you?" Morris spoke in reasonable, measured tones with an underlying firmness. "You know if we do, we'll lose everything we have here."

"We've already lost our water," Cheryl responded. With that comment, Slim looked up again at her with a cross scowl, and Cheryl recoiled a bit. Summoning her courage, she continued, "Slim. Morris. Please. You know this drought has no end in sight. The well levels are lower than ever. Fluoride is higher than ever! And that could mean a lot of danger for everyone!"

"Fluoride!" Slim scoffed. "When has fluoride ever hurt anybody?"

"I'm convinced there's a hazard," Cheryl asserted.

"How can we be sure the Colorado River water that the state wants to pipe in is any safer than our own mineral water?" said Morris, shaking his head in frustration.

As much as the mayor hated to admit it, the questions Slim and Morris asked were valid. Studies had failed to offer any conclusive evidence about the true toxicity of fluoride. But because of its metallic content, there was no telling what fluoride might do to the human body if digested in significant amounts. For this reason, government agencies thought it best to regulate fluoride consumption, at least until additional research could be finalized. Part of the plan to pipe in water from the Colorado River included the hope that the fluoride controversy would die.

So, regardless of objections from Kominsky, Wiggins, and many other town residents, the costly Elsinore Valley water project moved forward and was completed in July 1956. State officials and contractors promised the townspeople relief from the drought and an end to fluoride woes.

But the woes continucd, and new ones arose. Imported water threatened businesses that relied solely on the springs, including bathhouses, spas, pools, motels, and other tourist attractions. The controversies threw the entire town into division and utter conflict. City officials declared victory, whereas business owners declared war. Tempers were hot and many times flared out of control. Accusations rattled out like machine-gun fire back and forth across the valley, and there were no easy answers.

As time passed, each side entrenched and compromise faded further and further from reach. Even worse, each side had loud and proud doomsayers frightening anyone within hearing range.

"How can we compromise with an evil regime that has betrayed and repressed us!" Morris preached to everyone who would listen. And many listened.

With local businesses dying, tourism declining, residents leaving, and tax revenue dwindling, city administrators were stuck in an unforgiving impasse. On one hand, a huge investment had been made to route imported water to a thirsty land, and California officials felt good about that. On the other hand, what benefit did it offer if people were leaving town and no one was left to enjoy the new water supply? Like it or not, even government officials had to admit that the future of Elsinore depended on its mineral springs.

But the mineral water was unsafe, according to the State Department of Public Health.

Only an act of God could rectify the impossible situation. Unfortunately, years of drought left little hope for that. Rain was needed. Not just drizzles, but downpours.

Finally, in an effort to preserve the city and appease angry property owners, an attempt was made to dilute local water with the newly imported water from the Colorado River. The idea seemed reasonable, and perhaps even brilliant, but the results were disastrous. Fluoride levels did indeed drop, but there were unexpected consequences. Combining the waters produced a murky mixture that no one wanted to drink, bathe in, or look at. The water looked no better than the greenish duck pond on Slim Wiggin's ranch.

The watery concoction was deemed adequate for consumption, but the grim appearance did little to convince the citizens of Elsinore. Nor did tourism improve, which angered business owners further, causing their confidence in public administrators to continue to plummet. Most citizens began to believe that city bigwigs were more toxic to the community than fluoride was. It was obvious to them that politics was taking priority over people. If anything required cleansing it was the downtown council offices. Businessmen working on solutions were needed, not bureaucrats working on resumes.

Those in the community knew that they needed some muscle against the power of the state system, so the Elsinore Property Owners Association was established. Morris acted fast to nominate himself as chairman. Because of his unique background, he understood politics and all the red tape wrapped around it. As it turned out, however, his extreme alarmist disposition didn't always serve him well.

Throughout his life, Morris had always taken an inordinate interest in challenging authority, especially those people who were not aligned with his political views. And in 1950s America, very few were in line with his views.

Morris Kominsky was not hesitant to share his convictions either. In his past he had run for Governor of his home state of Rhode Island. He had campaigned as a candidate of the loathed Communist Party USA. With only a few hundred votes to boast of, Morris lost by a wide margin to the popular Republican William Henry Vanderbilt III. That earlier political slaughter failed to quiet Morris, however. As a freelance writer, he made it his mission to take down any capitalistic governing power that got in his crosshairs.

In time, Morris relocated his base of operations to Southern California. Here he not only made a name for himself, he also caught the eyes of investigators at the California Senate Factfinding Subcommittee on Un-American Activities (SUAC), and Morris welcomed the attention. In his mind, it served as a platform and opportunity to expose his fiercest enemies.

To his credit, Morris carried a burden for the oppressed. As a postwar Jew, he understood what it was like to be despised. This stirred within him a compassion for those beaten down by prejudice. Morris demanded a fair shake for all mankind regardless of race, ethnicity, or gender. He was an advocate for the poor and their need for government assistance. Living in a social and economic environment where not all were treated equal, these concerns were shared by many.

Most people couldn't go along with Morris when he proposed communism as the ultimate solution. People were still too aware of communism's long history of bloodshed, brutality, and oppression. Nevertheless, business owners in Elsinore needed a strong and outspoken leader with unique abilities and experience. The townspeople's zeal for justice blinded them from seeing that Morris's radical leanings might constitute a threat to their community and their cause.

Kominsky had all the tools needed to make heads roll among that small crowd sitting in comfortable city seats. So, as long as no red flags of communism were waved, Elsinore's property owners would continue to rally and fight for their mineral water. And instigator Morris Kominsky would lead the way.

5
Cold War

The year 1957 ushered in a bumper crop of news stories for journalists and their readers, listeners, and viewers to harvest. The Baby-Boomer birth rate had risen to an all-time peak. The king of Rock 'n Roll was establishing his glitzy Tennessee throne in Graceland, and Chevy sedans were growing taller, fancier tailfins.

The Space Age also commenced in 1957. Russian communists soared into an early lead with the launch of Sputnik I, the first artificial Earth satellite. This low-orbit object sported four antennas that broadcasted detectable pulses heard by radio amateurs around the globe. President Eisenhower responded to Sputnik by establishing the U.S. National Aeronautic and Space Administration (NASA), and rocket scientists around the United States rushed to enter the Space Race.

Concurrently, Pat Michaels was broadcasting his own brand of radio pulses faster than the Associated Press could deliver special alerts.

"In other leading news from Arkansas…" Pat barked fiercely into his radio microphone, "The Little Rock Nine are now sitting comfortably in class at Central High School, while President Eisenhower remains on the hot seat."

The Little Rock Nine, a group of African American teenagers, had been prevented from attending racially segregated Little Rock Central High School by order of State Governor Orval Faubus. After Faubus deployed the Arkansas National Guard to block the nine, Eisenhower sent 1000 U.S. Army paratroopers to ensure the students' safe passage on registration day.

"Navigating through an angry mob of protestors..." Pat continued his broadcast, "The Little Rock Nine successfully registered in a traditionally all-white campus. We have not heard the last on this story. The president must answer for deploying troops against fellow Americans. It is the opinion of this reporter that this was a step too far."

Deploying troops for the sake of nine African American youths was not President Ike's first brush with controversy. As a staunch Republican, Eisenhower countered the "noninterventionism" of his more pacifistic opponents by leading the crusade against "Communism, Korea, and Corruption." His stance was assertively hawkish, whereas liberal politicians wanted to roll out the "red" carpet for Marxist dictators.

In Ike's day, communism was as real as racism. As Martin Luther King Jr. marched for racial equality, communists marched for superiority whenever and wherever possible, leaving a long trail of blood from the Eastern Block, into Asia, and all the way into the Middle East. Because they were gaining ground and increasing in strength, Eisenhower called for aid to Mideast countries that were resisting armed aggression from communist-controlled nations.

As much as he opposed communism, Ike also rejected the "Russians are coming" fearmongering of McCarthyism. It became apparent that the "Senate Factfinding Subcommittees of UnAmerican Activities" didn't always have their facts straight, and this was true at both the state and federal levels. Too often, investigations were nothing more than witch-hunts, for which Ike had zero tolerance. Nevertheless, the president's criticisms of SUAC did little to lessen the nation's fears.

The threat of communism coupled with the reality of racism became forces to be reckoned with in the Land of the Free. These two issues alone created enough thunder for a perfect storm to gather. Eisenhower stood directly in the eye of it, shaking his angry fist and barking commands as if he were an Old Testament prophet who had authority over wind and sea. No dark cloud could move him.

All the while, journalists stood and watched from afar, primarily viewing Ike's battles as opportunities for sensational reporting, better ratings, and personal aggrandizement. Ike was a one-of-kind newsmaker. His courageous and controversial actions kept reporters such as Pat Michaels on their toes and at the top of their game.

Pat saw rainbows in the midst of all the storms swirling around Eisenhower. If Ike could be considered a prophet standing against the wind, Pat was an apostle. And it was up to this apostle to spread all the news—good, bad, true, exaggerated, or contrived.

Like the beeping pulses from an orbiting Sputnik, the miracle of radio propagated Pat's viewpoints around the world.

6
Suspicious Minds

The two men were hunched as usual in their rocking chairs at The Chimes, hating life, breathing each other's pungent pipe tobacco, and plotting. Morris complained about everything wrong with tap water and how it was killing Elsinore business. And Slim nodded his long, narrow face in complete agreement. How could he disagree? The owners of the popular Lakeside Inn had just announced that they were shutting their doors that very morning. They weren't the first nor would they be the last.

"They say fluoride is the reason for cutting off our mineral water," Morris scoffed. "But the real reason is obvious."

"And what would that be?" said Slim, raising his eyebrows.

"Put your thinking cap on, Slim," Morris answered tapping his forehead. "All those folks who had to close up shop, what do they have in common?"

Slim rubbed his chin, lost in thought.

"Come on, Slim. Think about it," coaxed Morris.

"Well," drawled Slim. "Um…I…"

Morris relit his pipe and breathed out a puff of smoke. "Slim, you need a hint?" he said. "I'll just rattle off a few names for you. Schwartz, Dreyfus, Bernstein, Epstein…"

Slowly the light dawned in Slim's head. "Lordy," he said, astonished. "They're all Jewish!"

"Bingo!"

"Are you saying there's some kind of government conspiracy to drive Jews out of Elsinore?"

"I don't need to say anything," Morris nodded. "The facts speak for themselves."

Anti-Semitism raised its ugly head in biblical days when Father Abraham had sent Hagar packing with their misbegotten son Ishmael. Sadly, this hatred has plagued our globe ever since, from nation to nation, to every generation. A rosy view of history would paint the Fabulous Fifties in America as a time when anti-Semitism was absent, but the truth is different.

As Jews emigrated to every known corner of the earth, so did Jew haters, and Elsinore was no exception. Nevertheless, government watchdogs in the 1950s were more concerned with communist radicals, such as Morris Kominsky, than they were with a few Jews leaving town.

During this time, Morris rattled enough cages at city hall with his anti-Semitism claims to keep SUAC watchdogs sniffing at his heels. Investigators were quick to dismiss his allegations as "heightened sensitivity among a predominately Jewish population." SUAC claimed that anti-Semitism was not a motivating factor for shutting off the mineral water, and there was no organized effort to drive Jews out of the area.

Not everyone in Elsinore shared SUAC's opinions. As the Jewish population dwindled, suspicions increased proportionately. Concurrently, the state agency grew increasingly suspicious of Morris Kominsky and his associates.

"Bureaucrats can deny it all they want," Morris spouted off to Slim. "It's what we believe that matters. The citizens of Elsinore can decide for themselves why it's only Jewish-owned businesses that are being shut down."

"Folks may not even realize this is happening," Slim deduced.

"Word spreads quickly around here," Morris assured. "With a little effort on our part, we can have the entire population convinced."

"We can post signs!" Slim suggested as he tried to keep up with the vision. "Let's expose this fluoride cover-up and tell everyone the real truth behind it!"

"I'm meeting with the property owners this evening," Morris replied. "I'll lay out a game plan."

It wasn't long before the whole town was talking about racism and discrimination against Jews. Many were quick to believe that Jews were targets of foul play, blaming local officials for cooperating in a sinister plot to oust them. Others adamantly rejected the notion, charging Morris and property owners with fueling a false narrative. The normally tight-knit community of Elsinore was splitting faster than peanut shells at happy hour, and the local media jumped into the fray with both feet.

The local Elsinore newspaper sided with town officials, refuting all allegations against them. Council members maintained they were looking out for children and sparing them from fluoride dangers. As concerned citizens scanned these news articles, they were forced to read between the lines to determine where the true evils lurked. Was it Jewish citizens who needed protection, or was it Elsinore's precious youth? In a culture where four kids per family was the norm, loyalties shifted like the wind.

To their credit, the city's official board had demographic diversity in its favor. Unlike most jurisdictions of the day, Elsinore had not fallen into the hands of an "all white male" administration. Although no Jews could be counted among the members, blacks and Hispanics did serve on the city council. And with Cheryl French presiding as Elsinore's first female mayor, it was hard to conceive that a multicultural team such as this would be intolerant of any minority group. This small town was years ahead of most districts that were colorful in community only, but not in representation.

Although allegations of anti-Semitism remained a matter of debate, the case in favor of spring water remained strong. Businesses couldn't survive without it. Property owners, however, lacked the media support that city officials used to their advantage.

Recognizing the power of the press, a writer with the pseudonym "Frank Observer" began reporting the property owners' viewpoints in a regular feature column in the *San Jacinto Valley Time*s. The widespread publication of this column not only increased subscription revenue for that newspaper, it also exacerbated the conflict within the community and beyond.

Frank's true identity remains a mystery to this day. Some suspect Morris Kominsky was the writer—a reasonable guess because Morris earned his living as a freelance writer and contributed to the most radical of periodicals. And, like Morris, Frank Observer maintained great fervor for the communist cause.

Two rival newspapers were now reporting from the battlefront, and many times they were engaging in the battle themselves. The war between property owners and council members had officially gone public, promising media moguls the biggest win of all. As long as tensions soared, the newspapers kept flying off the stands.

7

The Mouse That Roared

"Son, do you see that?" said Pat as he pointed to the night sky. "That's not only history in the making, it's the future of space travel!" But the scientific wonders of the universe didn't interest one-year-old Terrance who was snuggling in his mother's arms.

Pat had gathered the six members of the Michaels family high atop the San Bernardino Mountains, where the silent moonlight spilled down on a beautiful Lake Arrowhead vista. There they watched Sputnik I as it passed among the stars.

"One day we'll walk on the moon," Pat predicted, his eyes fixed on the tiny dot of light moving overhead.

"When can we hear the beeping?" said his oldest daughter Kathleen.

"Be patient!" shouted Pat.

It was unimaginable that an object no bigger than a beach ball could capture the attention of the entire world, but that's what was happening. Sputnik I revolved around the earth, reminding humanity that the Russians were the frontrunners in these early days of the international Space Race.

"Listen now," came the announcement on the NBC radio network, "for the sound that forevermore separates the old from the new." Listeners then heard the faint pitch that the Associated Press described as the Soviet satellite's "deep beep-beep." All ears in America listened intently as pulses from the atmosphere were transmitted from station to station.

There was no doubt that the chirp from space was a scientific marvel. But it also dismayed many Westerners living in the midst of the Cold War. The noise was a dreaded reminder that the Russians had already taken the lead on the technological battlefront. For this reason, the kerosene-powered Sputnik became known as The Mouse that Roared.

Whether his audience felt threatened or thrilled, Pat Michaels remained on top of the story, rebroadcasting the "deep beep-beep" at the beginning of every hour. After all, this event wasn't just any news; it was the primary story of 1957.

"No event since Pearl Harbor set off such repercussions in public life," wrote historian Walter McDougall in *The Heavens and the Earth—A Political History of the Space Age.* Sputnik I had successfully delivered a blow to American pride and confidence. At the same time, its subtle chirps provoked unprecedented media frenzy. The period became known not only as an era of space racing, but also of news chasing. Journalists fought each other for the best vocational opportunities and the largest audiences, directing the world's attention whenever possible away from mundane workaday pursuits toward fantastic space-age imaginings.

As news of the beeping satellite made major headlines, a heightened awareness swept the nation of the ever-growing presence of communism. With each "deep beep-beep" a subliminal message echoed, which U.S. patriots interpreted as "the Russians are coming." This fed further media madness; America had already survived the hyperparanoid ills of McCarthyism during which time scores of entertainers, writers, and broadcasters were blacklisted because of alleged communistic involvement.

And now, Sputnik I scoffed at America from the skies, promising an encore of still greater evil. And if that wasn't bad enough, the subsequent launch of Sputnik II drew even more attention.

"The Soviets have sent a dog into space!" Pat excitedly announced to KWIZ listeners.

It was true. The "deep beep-beep" was replaced by a helpless "woof woof." Laika, a female, part-Samoyed terrier, became the first living creature blasted into orbit. The dog didn't survive long. The pressurized cabin of the space capsule provided ample oxygen, food, and water, but it lacked climate control. Temperatures rapidly rocketed to more than 100 degrees, which killed the dog. Although Laika died quickly, the Soviets deemed their mission a success, reminding America once again of the USSR's huge lead in the Space Race.

Because of the additional fear fueled by Sputnik II, President Eisenhower asked his Science Advisory Committee to evaluate human survival in the nuclear age. The Security Resources Panel prepared the Gaither Report, which called for increased numbers of American missiles and fallout shelters.

Media responded to the report, publicizing the alarming concern that the Soviets possessed all the necessary technology to launch ballistic missiles and wipe out the United States in a nuclear holocaust.

And then even more news of communism hit the headlines. On November 15, 1957, Pat Michaels reported the sentencing of Soviet spy Vilyam Genrikovich Fisher, better known by his alias Rudolf Ivanovich Abel. Fisher worked undercover for the KGB as part of a spy ring in New York City. The covert mission was to collect military secrets and to secure documents about U.S. plans to develop nuclear weapons. These plans were known as the Manhattan Project.

Because of Fisher's excessive drinking, he left a sloppy trail that led to his capture. His arrest served as another sobering reminder of a Soviet threat. It also gave Pat an idea for a story.

"We need to go to Fremont tomorrow," Pat informed his wife.

"Hasn't that story been covered enough?" Lois asked. "Besides, the kids were bored last time. They've seen enough bomb blasts on TV."

"I'm not interested in nuclear-bomb testing this time," Pat told her. "This time I'm testing something myself! I want to see how easy it is to get past security."

"Why on earth would you want to do that?"

"If a communist like Fisher can gain access to federally secured areas, that's a big problem, and it needs to be fixed!"

"What if you get arrested?" Lois exclaimed with shock.

"I'm a reporter, not a spy," Pat reasoned.

54

Mr. and Mrs. Michaels and their kids weren't the only ones traveling to Freemont, Nevada. The atomic-bomb testing site drew thousands to the area. Those in neighboring Las Vegas were thankful for the additional tourist revenue. City hotels remained full, serving as ready lookout posts for those wanting to view the gigantic mushroom clouds blooming over the desert. This time, however, Pat wasn't just another spectator. Pat was on an undercover mission.

"I got in without a press card," He announced triumphantly on his broadcast the following day. "All it took was a free drink coupon from the local bar!"

He wasn't lying. Pat schmoozed his way past security with a smile and the offer of a cocktail. He also made headlines by doing so. It was terrific publicity for him, but not for the nuclear-testing site. Government security personnel demanded a quick fix, and any problems in Fremont were immediately corrected.

But in Elsinore, the troubles continued to increase.

8
Tall Tales

It wasn't just fluoride lurking in the waters. Many years previously, Native Americans of the Elsinore Valley recounted the story of a sea monster that swam through the depths of Southern California's largest natural lake. Named "Elsie" by twentieth-century residents, the creature was described as a cross between a sea serpent and a plesiosaur—perhaps a distant cousin to the Loch Ness Monster of the Scottish highlands. The California leviathan raised her massive head at least once a decade.

The first sighting of Elsie was recorded in 1884. Then in 1932, rancher C.B. Greenstreet claimed he had spotted her again. Greenstreet described Elsie as "100 feet long with a thirty foot tail." His wife and children, who were with him that day, described "waves as high as light posts" crashing on the lake's normally tranquil shores.

This sort of report made believers of many. But the tales appeared bogus in 1954 after the rain stopped; explorers in the cracked lakebed found no trace of a sea monster.

Some said that Elsie had crawled out of the lakebed during the drought to wait in a cave for the water to flow again. When the water did finally return, so apparently did Elsie, as sightings were documented in 1967, 1970, and 1992. So the fearful legend continued.

Just as Elsie surfaced periodically from the waters of Lake Elsinore, so the shadowy menace of communism appeared more and more frequently in the 1950s, and the perceived communist threat grew with each sighting.

Communism was neither myth nor legend. It was real. Communists were fewer in the western hemisphere than elsewhere around the globe, but there was enough Red Threat in the United States to keep Elsinore on official watch lists.

According to one SUAC report, "The infiltration and agitation at Elsinore had its inception in 1946 with the formation of the Elsinore Progressive League, a Negro organization with a few white members, conceived and operated by the Communist Party. Its secretary was Mrs. R.L. Burks, and during the period of its active operation from 1946 to 1955, it exerted a considerable influence in the community and the adjacent vicinity and constituted a nucleus for the spreading of the infection. The Elsinore Progressive League was designated by the Attorney General of the United States as a Communist-dominated organization on October 20, 1955, and on November 1 of that year."

It was further noted that at least thirty-six Elsinore residents subscribed to publications known for "the spreading of the most vicious kind of Communist propaganda." In comparing *The National Guardian* to two separate communist rags, SUAC warned, "it has outstripped both of the others combined in its tirade of Communist propaganda, abuse against our government and our cherished institutions, in an obvious effort to discredit public confidence in our official representatives."

Attention was also given to *The Morning Freiheit* a Jewish publication and counterpart to *The National Guardia*n. It had ten subscribers in Elsinore, most notably Morris Kominsky.

The SUAC report also mentioned James McGowan, who operated a radio and TV-repair business on the outskirts of Elsinore. It was noted that McGowan "took an active part in the Elsinore Property Owners Association from the very inception of the difficulty, and was frequently observed in open and covert conferences with its leading lights, especially Morris Kominsky."

McGowan never tried to hide his true beliefs. In 1947 he ran for city council in the 11th District of Los Angeles as a proud representative of the Communist Party. He also campaigned in favor of several other candidates seeking public office on the communist ticket.

In the early 1940s, McGowan had lived in Tulare, California, where he served as "executive secretary of the Communist Party for all of Tulare County and the cities of Hanford and Corcoran in adjacent Kings County."

The SUAC report further added that, "[McGowan] was elected to this position about a week after arriving in the county at a meeting which was held at a private home in the City of Tulare." During this period, James McGowan had been called before the senate to answer for these and other suspicious activities.

With McGowan and Kominsky already under the watchful eyes of both the Attorney General and SUAC, they weren't the best picks to represent the Elsinore property owners, whose general predisposition was toward obeying the law. Yet these die-hard communists were chosen as the chief strategists to direct the community organization.

The grievances of the property owners were valid, but their motives now were increasingly suspect. Every move by Kominsky and McGowan hinted of conspiracy.

Like a dark, dripping reptile looming from a choppy lake, the fear of communism continued rearing its head in Elsinore.

9

Space Dog

"If you observe a small spacecraft flying overhead this evening..." Pat announced during his five o'clock broadcast, "Be sure to wave. Laika just might be watching!"

The Soviets never reported that their astronaut hound had died within hours of takeoff. They had convinced the world that she was still enjoying the ride of her life, as if she were headed to a dog park in the back of a pickup truck with her tail wagging and tongue flapping in the breeze. Even without a pulse, Laika's fame was surpassing that of canine TV star Rin Tin Tin—at least for a brief time.

As long as people believed Laika was alive, fascination with the mission continued. But if Laika's true condition became known, the Soviets would lose the advantage in the Space Race that they had secured. That was the cold reality of it. The fate of Sputnik II rested in the stiff paws of a cooked canine.

The real mission of Sputnik II was to prove whether a living creature could survive after being launched into orbit. Laika, a stray from the streets of Moscow, was the ideal guinea pig. Although she was expected to live longer than she did, her rendezvous with death was certain. Sputnik II was designed to shoot a living creature into space, but there was no provision for return. So Laika was chosen to make the ultimate sacrifice for Soviet science.

Oleg Gazenko, one of the scientists responsible for Laika's fatal space ride, later lamented, "We shouldn't have done it... We did not learn enough from this mission to justify the death of the dog."

Oblivious to Laika's true condition, Pat covered the Sputnik story with great interest from beginning to end. With every broadcast, his fascination with space travel soared to new heights. If possible, he would have happily volunteered to be the first American astronaut blasted into outer space. But if that weren't practical, the next best thing would be to own his own aircraft. Pat just wanted to fly, that's all.

And why shouldn't Pat fly? It was an era when man was accomplishing the unimaginable, pushing past previous limitations and boundaries, and ignoring people who said, "it's never been done before!" The sky was the limit, or maybe even beyond the sky! There was no reason for anybody to remain on the sidelines, not even an aspiring reporter.

So it was settled—at least in Pat's mind. Pat determined he would get his pilot's license as soon as possible.

"Come on, Lois. This is the jet age! We have to keep up with the times. Besides, all the other journalists in the neighborhood have airplanes!" Pat joked.

Lois didn't laugh. "Oh, Pat. There are just so many other things we need. An airplane isn't practical. What on earth would we do with one?"

"Escape in the middle of the night if we needed to," he laughed. "Just like we did in New Orleans a few years ago." The year was 1953 to be exact.

"Never again!" she threatened. "We barely got out with the clothes on our backs, let alone our children."

Lois turned back to washing dishes in the sink as Pat chuckled and refocused on reading his newspaper at the kitchen table. He rattled the pages to straighten them, and Lois looked down at the soapy water. Her mind drifted back to those frightening days on the Gulf Coast as she placed a plate in the rack to drain.

During the time the family was in New Orleans, Lois had no idea how urgent the situation had become. As usual, Pat didn't communicate much. But as it turned out, the Michaels were lucky to get out of the city alive.

After reporting on police corruption in the French Quarter, Pat was met one night in the studio parking lot by Sergeant Edward Touzet, who threatened him at gunpoint. The next day, Pat reported the incident to Aaron Kohn, chief investigator of the Special Citizens Investigative Committee. Kohn was on his own mission to rid New Orleans of dirty cops.

Because of their shared interests, Kohn had become a regular guest on Pat's TV broadcasts on WDSU. On the show, Kohn named names all the way up the chain of command in the police department, along with a few corrupt politicians.

Several days after the gun incident, Pat received a phone call at his house.

"You better not interview Kohn on your little TV show any more, Mr. Pat Michaels. Otherwise your family might start disappearing one by one!"

The incident in the parking lot was bad enough, but the threatening phone call pushed Pat into action. He told Lois about the call, and the Michaels family wasted no time. They packed their belongings and disappeared into the hot, humid night.

The memories flooded back, and surface tension held a quivering tear at the corner of Lois's eye. She wiped it with a dishcloth and turned toward her husband.

"You don't need an airplane," she was tempted to say. "You need a muzzle!" Fearing Pat's violent temper, Lois held back her tongue.

Pat heard Lois sigh deeply and he looked at her blankly, uncomprehending.

10
Water War

Near the end of 1957, dark clouds gathered over Lake Elsinore and finally brought rain to the drought-stricken basin. Several weeks later, a modest eight feet of water covered the bottom of the gorge. It wasn't enough for Elsie the sea monster to swim in, but it was a promising start, and Elsinore residents prayed for more precipitation.

Rain refreshed the thirsty mineral wells, too. As water levels rose, fluoride concentration decreased. The dropping levels of fluoride didn't satisfy city and state legislators, however. Refusing to budge in their support for tap water, legislators continued making their case against fluoride, insisting that imported water was safer for consumption than water from the local springs.

Legislators were obliged to support the piped-in water because millions of dollars and countless man-hours had already been expended on the Colorado River pipeline, and they could not abandon this newly implemented distribution network. On the contrary, its existence had to be justified.

As it turned out, the blessing of rain in Elsinore brought with it a greater curse. The rising lake level did nothing to soothe tensions among property owners and public officials; it made tensions worse. Offended businessmen ratcheted up their rhetoric against city bigwigs, and officials became more defensive. As the end of the drought appeared nearer, the dam of indignation was about to burst.

"It's just not right," Morris ranted to James McGowan. "We now have viable spring water and it's still off limits, thanks to these government morons!"

"Yeah," McGowan agreed.

"The mayor says what's done is done, and there's no turning back," Morris scoffed. "Humph! That's garbage!"

"Maybe she doesn't think she can turn things back," James said. "But she doesn't know what we're capable of. Let's give them the full-throated Red Scare and show them what we're really all about!"

"Whoa, James. We have to be cautious," Morris warned. "We can't frighten those in our own camp."

"Good point," James concurred. "But we've lost momentum now that we've had some rain. How do we motivate the property owners again? Even our own propaganda machine needs some oiling now."

"It's time to flex our muscle again," Morris declared. "Somehow, we need to overtake City Hall."

"I agree," James nodded. "Only then will we have complete control of our water."

"There's one thing we need to do first."

"What's that?"

"Sue the pants off every last person responsible for this mess!"

"That's a great idea!" James smiled broadly. "I'm certain the property owners in the POA will back us up!"

As predicted, the idea of a lawsuit was met with enthusiasm at the next POA meeting. After all the losses the people had suffered, compensation seemed only fair. James passed out pens and papers to each member, and everyone tallied up estimates of accumulated damages. Morris collected the stack.

"All in favor of compiling the complaints of aggrieved property owners to create a lawsuit and/or lawsuits against state and local government officials, say aye!" Morris bellowed.

"Aye," came the unanimous response. The excitement was palpable and righteous indignation was rekindled in the home and business owners' hearts. They weren't whipped yet. They would rise again to correct the many terrible wrongs perpetrated against them.

So the motion was approved, and the wheels of justice began grinding inexorably toward the day when this major lawsuit would be served.

Morris Kominsky felt invigorated. He wasted no time in seeking the legal representation of his friend, Attorney Guy Downing. "I need your help, Guy," said Morris. "And this one should pay off handsomely for you!"

"What can I do for you, old friend?" said Guy, his ears perking up at the sound of cash.

Morris explained the case to Downing, making repeated mention of the fact that the court action included a number of written guarantees, in which the government stated there would be no disruption of mineral water during the Colorado River project.

"The city council guaranteed this in writing?" Downing asked with surprise.

"They absolutely did! I swear!" Morris claimed.

"I assume these guarantees are signed on government letterhead?"

"You assume rightly," Morris assured.

"Then we've got a slam dunk case! I'm your man, Morris!"

From that moment on, Downing exhibited his characteristic grit and vigor as he prepared the property owners' action against the government. Those named in the suit included Elsinore's City officials and others responsible for the promotion and formation of the water district. Council members were accused of deliberately cutting off Elsinore's mineral water without warning for businesses that were solely reliant on it.

To compensate for previous losses, and to prevent further losses, a court order was sought for full restoration of the mineral water. And the plaintiffs were claiming $5,000,000 in damages.

The claim landed in the council offices like a bomb, causing much anxiety in City Hall. And when the bureaucrats read the names of the notorious men filing as primary claimants, their heartburn increased. The names of Morris Kominsky and James McGowan stuck out like communist flags in a U.S. color guard.

With Elsinore already on the watch-list for communist activity, California Senator Hugh M. Burns was soon alerted about the situation. At the time of the lawsuit, Burns was serving as acting chairman of SUAC. Coincidentally, he was also the recognized father of the State Water Project and the author of the bond issue used to fund its creation. Thus Burns took a personal interest in the Elsinore matter. He was alarmed, and he initiated further investigations.

"The situation in Elsinore is escalating," Senator Burns told his investigative team. "We need our people out there at once."

"I can smell the Reds from here," answered Agent Van Dussell. "Count me in."

Suspicions were confirmed. The communist influence was alive and well in Elsinore, albeit on a small scale thus far. The power of communism was growing in muscle, however, and it was further determined that the registered communists serving at the helm of the Elsinore Property Owners Association were a danger to state—and possibly to national—security.

Several items in the lawsuit raised the eyebrows of investigators. Not only did the suit hint of the hammer and sickle, but there also was no proof of any "written guarantees" promising an uninterrupted supply of mineral water. These so-called "attached exhibits," to which the claim repeatedly referred, were nowhere to be found. Investigators notified the county clerk that the complaint was defective without them. The clerk contacted Attorney Guy Downing.

"I'll get those documents right over to you," said Guy.

Downing hung up the phone and immediately picked it up again to dial Morris's number.

"Hello?" said Morris.

Guy couldn't contain his irritation. "Kominsky!" he shouted. "Where the blue blazes are those doggone government guarantees?"

11
UFO

"Not only do we have a dog in outer space…" Pat announced. "An unidentified flying object has been sighted in Levelland, Texas. This late-breaking story comes to us from KDFW in Dallas/Fort Worth."

Pat muted his mic, took a long drag from his cigarette, and flicked a half-inch of ash into a butt-filled tray. He loved his Kents and he regarded a smoke-filled broadcast booth as heaven on earth. In a strange way smoking validated him. It was an age when cigarettes were as important to reporters as press badges.

"There are at least fifteen witnesses," Pat continued. "Including the Levelland sheriff!"

In the late 1950s, when four-legged creatures were orbiting the earth, flying saucers didn't seem farfetched. This was the Space Age, after all.

Riding on the coattails of this cosmic fascination was the Mormon Church with their claim that God ruled from outer space on the planet Kolob—this according to the Book of Abraham, published by Latter Day Saints' prophet Joseph Smith. By the end of 1957, nearly 72,000 new converts to Mormonism had accepted the idea of an intergalactic deity, propelling the number of LDS adherents to a million and a half in America. This served to confirm a growing obsession with interplanetary travel and the Great Beyond.

Even those who found Mormon theology laughable took UFOs seriously. Orson Welles had proved this point in 1938 with his radio broadcast of The War of the Worlds, during which hundreds of panicked Americans believed that Martians were attacking New Jersey.

Orson Welles had adapted his radio play from a novel by H.G. Wells, but Pat read from an actual news script hot off the Associated Press. Accounts of the weird craft in Texas were astonishingly similar. In each instance, eyewitnesses heard a rush of wind, followed by a flash of blue light, and then a strong wave of heat. Out of the blue glow, an egg-shaped rocket emerged, estimated by some to be at least 200 feet long. It roared like thunder. Those in vehicles all claimed that their engines instantly died, along with their batteries, lights, and radios.

Texas Tech student Newell Wright stated that his "car engine began to sputter, the ammeter on the dash jumped to discharge and then back to normal, and the motor started cutting out like it was out of gas… the car rolled to a stop; then the headlights dimmed and in several seconds went out." When he got out to check on the problem Newell saw a "100-foot long" egg-shaped object sitting in the road, and then he watched it take off into the night sky. After the UFO was gone, his car returned to normal.

Local police received more than a dozen calls describing similar incidents, all within a few hours on the same evening. When Sheriff Weir Clem investigated, he saw a brilliant red object moving across the sky. Barely fifteen minutes later, Fire Chief Ray Jones called in a similar report, claiming his vehicle engine had sputtered out.

"The Levelland UFO case is currently under investigation by the U.S. Air Force," Pat said as he wrapped up his broadcast that night. "Keep your dial tuned to KWIZ for late-breaking updates."

Having smoked the Kent down to a nub, Pat took a final nasty drag and ground the filter into the overflowing tray. He reached into his jacket pocket and pulled out the nearly empty pack. He lit the last cigarette and took a puff.

In the smoky fog, Pat wondered what strange thing those people in Levelland might be drinking. Or were the communists up to their devious tricks again? Or—dare he think it—was this giant egg really an alien craft from outer space?

He pushed back his chair and stood up. The cigarette tip flared red in the dimness, and he exhaled another cloud.

"These are exciting times for a radio newscaster!" he told himself.

Pat turned off the light, locked the door behind him, and walked downstairs to his Buick on the street.

He drove home in the dark.

12

Eleventh Report

Recognizing how potentially explosive the Elsinore situation was, California Senator Burns pursued his investigation cautiously, like a parent tiptoeing near the crib of a colicky napping infant. Burns knew that any appearance of peace in Elsinore was illusory and temporary.

Burly Senator Burns was built like a barrel with the neck of an ape. Despite his imposing girth, no Democratic Senator was as gentle as Hugh M. Burns. He normally shied away from conflicts and saw himself as a peacemaker. His peers on both sides of the political aisle respected his kindly demeanor. Visitors to the state capitol usually thought highly of him as well, after he treated them to a brandy coffee or two in his office. He exuded a calming influence when emotions ran high in others.

But Senator Burns needed all his patience, self-control, and wisdom during the probe for information in Elsinore. He discovered that fear and anger had swamped the town.

Burns arrived in Elsinore one afternoon in his black DeSoto. He stopped at the curb in front of City Hall, turned off the motor, and set the emergency brake. Taking a deep breath, he leaned back against the seat. For a long moment he looked up at the brown cloth on the car's ceiling.

"Wisdom, please," was all he said.

Burns started investigating, careful not to add fuel to the smoldering brands of revolution in the town. He decided he would reserve judgment against those involved, and he wouldn't embarrass any perceived communist agitators. These and other considerations were detailed in the California Legislature's *Eleventh Report of the Senate Fact-Finding Subcommittee on Un-American Activities*. As the enquiry unfolded, Senator Burns included this statement with his findings:

"...visits to Elsinore and the adjacent vicinity by Committee representatives disclosed an extremely complicated and challenging situation. Some evidence of Communist influence in the turbulent situation was discovered at an early date, but it was not deemed sufficient to warrant the holding of a hearing. At the same time there was evidence of anti-Semitism, political pressures and intrigue, economic factors, the prospects of a lengthy litigation in court and a pending city election— all of these elements making it extremely inexpedient for this Committee to inject itself into the situation until there was more time to make a searching and thorough investigation, allow the turbulence to settle, and to avoid any interference with the orderly conduct of the municipal election and the trial of the suit. It was accordingly determined that the investigation would be continued, and that no hearing would be held until after the election and answers to the complaint had been filed. Filing of answers to the complaint were delayed and the Committee soon discovered that it would take months of work to prepare any adequate background for the holding of a hearing."

In light of the reports, state authorities were wary about taking action. City officials needed time to answer the complaints against them. They were advised not to respond until Attorney Guy Downing had produced the missing exhibits—those so-called "written guarantees" that assured the uninterrupted flow of mineral water. Where were they? Did they even exist? Without these exhibits, city officials maintained a small hope that they might not lose everything.

The suit had been served nevertheless, and the defendants felt stranded and isolated in their offices. It was easy for them to imagine the townspeople taking up torches and pitchforks and storming City Hall, just as the peasants did in those horror movies starring Bela Lugosi—late actor and former Elsinore resident.

Mayor Cheryl French happened to be standing by her window that day when Burns drove up. Peeping through the venetian blinds, she recognized the famous senator as he lumbered out of his car.

Burns questioned the team, and the mayor and her council counterpunched. "We're right, they're wrong," was the overarching message Burns received from the politicians. "It's not fair! We were just trying to do what was right!"

French and her colleagues knew the accusations in the lawsuit were false, but fear and public disgrace haunted them and clouded their reason.

Days passed, and then weeks, and rumored written guarantees never appeared. As a result, the suit lapsed. "Hallelujah!" shouted Cheryl when she heard the news. She rushed out of her office to tell the others.

As it turned out, the problems in City Hall were far from resolved.

After the threat of the lawsuit had waned, the Property Owners Association tried other tactics to overthrow the local leaders. Rather than allow them to serve out their terms, the POA plotted to impeach them or hold a vote of no confidence. Morris and the POA demanded an immediate recall election, and most of the community rallied in support of these efforts. The mayor and councilmen were targeted, along with anyone else responsible for interrupting the flow of Elsinore's cherished mineral water, including even the security officer who guarded the shut-off valve.

To exacerbate the problems, Morris and James kept tossing around allegations of anti-Semitism. It was an effective campaign, and it left a dark cloud of suspicion hovering over Elsinore.

Reporters profited most from all the scandals. They turned in story after story, and printing presses clattered continuously. Newspapers flew off the stands as people hungrily read the latest gossip and thirsted for more.

Each day brought new revelations, and city officials squirmed in their swivel chairs, their fists clenched in indignation.

It was a hurricane. Burns had trouble maintaining his calm visage while he and his investigators were twisting around in the middle of it.

The maelstrom would also suck in Pat Michaels.

13
Project Blue Book

After tearing the latest newsfeed sheet from the AP Teletype, Pat hurried to the broadcast booth. With an unlit Kent between two fingers, he scanned through eight feet of Manila paper to find at least one item worth reporting. The brief blurb on the Elsinore lawsuit was of little concern to him, and he figured the story wouldn't interest anyone else either. He searched for bigger headlines. Finally, Pat grinned as he saw the story he was looking for. He tore the story apart from the rest. "This report is spookier than the movie previews of the horror film The *Screaming Skull*!" he said to himself gleefully.

"The U.S. government has now investigated the Levelland UFO case," Pat announced. "And prominent members of the press, such as myself, have carefully scrutinized these findings."

Pat enunciated his words carefully, using his best dramatic broadcaster's voice. Placing his free hand on his chest, he spoke deeply from his diaphragm and he avoided the higher registers of his vocal chords. Every syllable resonated perfectly in the smooth baritone he'd perfected through the years. The words "prominent members of the press" felt especially affirming to him. To add further richness, Pat drew close to the microphone, as if to kiss it. He could feel the cold metal shield brush against his lips. "Here are the official findings of Project Blue Book…"

Formed in 1947, Project Blue Book was the official U.S. Air Force branch tasked to research and investigate UFO sightings. After a brief visit to Levelland, the sergeant assigned to the case quickly dismissed reports of any encounters with alien crafts. Suspecting that thunderstorms were in the area on the night of the sightings, the sergeant concluded that the suspicious space object was most likely "ball lightening," otherwise known as "St. Elmo's Fire." The engine failures in various vehicles were attributed to "wet electrical circuits."

"Not everyone agrees with the conclusions of Project Blue Book," Pat informed his listeners. "The findings are challenged by many of Levelland's most notable citizens, including the law-enforcement officers who witnessed the strange events."

Judging by the investigators' attitudes, it was arguable that the researchers disbelieved the people's reports even before they arrived in the Texas town. As a result, the citizens considered their conclusions biased and nonobjective. It was clear that there was no appetite in the Air Force for a panic resulting from aliens landing in the Lone Star State, especially if the unexplained visitors could somehow be connected to the latest Russian advances in the Space Race. The investigation was wrapped up in a mere seven hours—virtually before it began.

The Air Force only interviewed three eyewitnesses. The first was Pedro Saucedo, an uneducated immigrant, and his testimony was immediately dismissed as unreliable.

"Saucedo's account could not be relied upon," the PBB report stated. "He had only a grade-school education, had no concept of direction, and was conflicting in his answers." These negative first impressions tainted the rest of the investigation, further dooming the inquiry.

Despite the government's downplaying of events, Pat's newshound nose smelled a story. How could so many eyewitnesses possibly make up all the sightings out of thin air?

"It should also be noted," Pat continued on air, "that there are no reports of electrical storms on the night of these sightings. Meteorologists must have had their eyes on Sputnik and not on the weather conditions."

For a brief second Pat muted the mic and sucked on his lit Kent. Pat didn't mention that he himself hadn't investigated the Levelland weather conditions either.

"And the U.S. Air Force must have had their eyes elsewhere, too, if they think there actually were storms around northwest Texas that night. Keep your radio dial on KWIZ for the latest in breaking updates as this story unfolds."

Pat flipped off the mic and finished his cigarette, pondering his latest performance. Perhaps there really is nothing to this Levelland story, he thought. Maybe it is just a hoax or a bunch of weird coincidences. Regardless, I'll keep this story alive and growing!

Pat knew how to create front-page news out of nothing.

14

Public Disturbance

SUAC maintained a steady eye on the Elsinore uprising, noting in their report, "Two years before the Elsinore trouble occurred, Morris Kominsky moved from Los Angeles to Elsinore and established his residence in that city. He immediately joined the Elsinore Valley Property Owners Association and was made its coordinator, investigator, propagandist, and spokesman. Immediately there was launched an intensive propaganda campaign that preceded the institution of the lawsuit. *The Valley Times*, formerly published in San Jacinto by James E. Lewis, was used as the vehicle for the Property Owners Association, their articles appearing in the 1957 issues for September 11, September 18, September 25, October 2, October 9, October 23, October 30, November 6, November 13, November 20, November 27, and December 4."

"I've been interviewed three times already," Morris complained to James McGowan. "Once by the D.A. and twice by senate investigators. They're not only on my tail, they're determined to find out who Frank Observer is."

"They tried to get me to talk, too," James huffed. "They suspect we're all masterminds of a communist plot."

"We need to be careful. They're watching our every move."

"Yeah. I'll be sure to let Frank Observer know!" James said, laughing sardonically.

The mysterious Frank Observer showed little regard for government watchdogs. Ignoring them completely, Frank concentrated on pillorying Elsinore's governmental officials, blaming them for the water war and every other scandal in Southern California during the past few years. In his article dated September 11, 1957, Observer wrote that the Colorado River water was "distributed through the Elsinore City Water System with disastrous results to the spa owners and indirectly to the economy of the entire area." Frank Observer further alleged, "The entire matter had been handled by the city administration summarily, secretly, and ineptly... spurred on by neurotics and psychotics on the lunatic fringe of our community."

In addition to these allegations, Observer asked readers to send letters demanding an "immediate resumption of mineral water delivery, sent through the medium of the Property Owners Association." On a separate page of the same issue, camp director and property owner Ben Kagan blasted Elsinore's local papers for refusing to publicize the POA's cause. Kagan instead saluted James Lewis, publisher of the San Jacinto Valley Times, for allowing Frank Observer to voice the righteous concerns of the citizens.

Observer's voice was heard clearly in James Lewis's newspaper. In one rant, the columnist described Elsinore's City Council as "connivers" and "hate peddlers" involved in a "deliberate conspiracy."

Mayor French read the news report and threw down the paper in disgust. "If that isn't the pot calling the kettle black!" she uttered, her brow furrowing with hurt and anger. "It's an attempt to take the suspicion off the state and lay it on us! Next thing you know, they'll blame us for putting the fluoride in the water in the first place!"

Sam Farber, a respected property owner and realtor, also weighed in on the matter. His letter appeared in the September 18 issue of the Valley Times. "Despite opinions to the contrary from the State Health Department, the mineral waters of Elsinore were chemically sound and entirely fit for human consumption," he opined.

The attacks continued on September 25, when even more irate letters were published. Thanks to Frank Observer's appeal, Elsinore residents not only tightened the noose in print on City Council, but they also called for a citywide telephone campaign to demand the immediate return of mineral water to the wells. During that time, council members' phones rang as many as eight times an hour, not just in their offices, even at their homes.

The perks of public service were quickly losing their allure, and several city representatives, including Councilman Webber, threatened to resign if the situations weren't resolved immediately.

"This is nothing short of harassment!" cried Cheryl French as the phone rang for the third time during her normally quiet dinner hour.

As the *San Jacinto Valley Times* continued its assault, Elsinore's local papers finally published some rebuttals. But the tidal wave of bad press from the *Valley Times* overwhelmed the local defenses.

Frank Observer lashed out even more fiercely on October 2. "There were glaring discrepancies between the accounts of the two Elsinore papers and a large Riverside paper concerning a meeting of the Elsinore City Council on September 23. The only true and reliable account to be found was printed in the *Valley Times*, as reported by the Property Owners Association."

Naturally, state investigators took issue with Frank Observer's analysis. They considered his articles part of an organized propaganda campaign spawned by communist agitators. Elsinore's citizens were dragged into the fray. For them, it was difficult to know who or what to believe. Most residents wanted the controversies to pass quickly, and removing some city officials seemed a logical solution. Stubborn property owners continued their campaign to do whatever necessary to restore their suffering town back to its former tranquil days of peace and prosperity, even though that dream seemed more and more impossible as time passed.

The telephone rang like a jagged knife in the night and Cheryl's eyes popped open. She grabbed in the dark for the phone on the nightstand. Her heart pounding, she pulled the phone cord from the wall.

It took almost an hour for Cheryl to fall asleep again that night. And when she did, Morris Kominsky and Slim Wiggins haunted her dreams.

15
Covert Affair

Residing in Orange County exposed Pat Michaels to many of Southern California's rich and famous people. When Pat wasn't reporting, he was hobnobbing at the prestigious Balboa Bay Club in Newport Beach. John Wayne, Doris Day, and other celebrities set his heart pounding like a groupie with a backstage pass. If one were to ask, Pat knew all of them well—even if they didn't know him at all.

As much as Pat pursued Hollywood's elite, it was the typewriter that stole his heart. To hear him hammer at the keys was like listening to nickels pile into a tin bucket from a slot machine. His passion for writing exploded from his fingertips like lightening. Radio was his first love, but the newspaper remained his mistress.

It was rare for Pat to seek news leads at the Bay Club. He knew better than to bother folks there. Then again, there were always exceptions. One afternoon he saw Attorney George Chula out of the corner of his eye, and he couldn't contain himself. He knew that talking to George was the equivalent of reading headlines in the making. Pat slid off his barstool and walked toward George's table. The next drink would be on Pat.

"Hey George! How're ya' doing?" he said, clapping the attorney on the shoulder."

George looked at Pat. "Oh. Hi Pat. I'm fine, thanks. How are you?"

"I see you got your name in the news again," Pat said with a chuckle. "Biggest drug bust on record I hear. Multiple arrests. How many of those creeps are you defending now?"

"I hope you're not fishing for info, Pat. That case is highly confidential. Press coverage is forbidden."

"Oh George, cut the company line. Give me something, brother," Pat cajoled. "A name. Something. Who tipped off the cops?"

"I can't give you a name. All I can say is that the cops had someone on the inside. She's the star witness."

"She?" Pat reacted with surprise.

George took a swig of scotch and squinted at Pat under bushy brows. He paused, debating between his professional obligation and his love of "off-the-record" gossip. Finally he opened his mouth. "Yes, Pat. She. A housewife, believe it or not. She got in real cozy with the head cheese. That's all I can say." George turned back to his drink.

Pat nodded. "Hey, I appreciate it, pal. I'll follow up with my connections downtown." Pat, anxious to track down his new lead, turned to walk away. But then he stopped and fished in his pocket. He pulled out a couple of bucks and dropped them on the table in front of Chula.

"Thanks, George. Have a drink on me. Please." George watched Pat as he walked out the door.

Pat did follow up the lead, and the trail led to an attractive homemaker who went by the pseudonym Lynn Stuart. She agreed to talk as long as her identity remained protected. Pat honored her request by conducting interviews at an undisclosed location. Lynn typically arrived wearing dark sunglasses and a scarf to cover her wavy blonde locks. The fruit of these meetings was more valuable than Pat had expected. After each meeting, he remained glued to his typewriter for hours, producing story after story about the perilous adventures of Lynn Stuart.

Lynn had lived in a run-down neighborhood in Santa Ana, and the rampant drug trafficking there increasingly disturbed her. Shady, untrustworthy characters roamed the streets at all hours, and she knew they didn't belong there. She worried most for her children. These thugs preyed on the neighborhood youth, profiting from the children's meager allowances and turning sweet kids into strung-out addicts.

"Something had to be done," Lynn explained to Pat. "The situation was out of control."

"What prompted your involvement?" Pat asked.

"The death of my two teenaged nephews," Lynn said bitterly. "They were driving my sister's car… high on dope—dope purchased right on my street! When cops tried to pull them over, they fled. They crashed after a high-speed chase. Both of the boys were killed instantly.

"I was devastated and angry, and I eventually decided to turn my grief into action. I volunteered as an undercover narcotics agent. Police initially thought the idea was absurd. They told me they wouldn't even think of throwing a homemaker into a pack of ravenous wolves. So they quickly rejected my offer."

"What made them change their minds?" Pat asked.

"To be honest, I had given up on the idea. The cops said they already had someone on the inside. Apparently he got found out. After his murder, they reconsidered my offer."

"Why you? Why not another undercover cop?"

"A woman is less suspicious, plus we smell prettier, I guess," said Lynn, looking out the window.

"Good point," Pat said, looking down at his notepad.

"I guess the cops thought that a womanly touch worked for Delilah, right? I mean, she turned on the female charm, and then Samson spilled the beans. Somehow I had to get close to Willie Down, the kingpin. There was no way around it. And I did get close, too…" Lynne paused. "After that… I heard and saw everything."

"How did the two of you meet?" Pat inquired.

"I was put to work at a diner where Willie and his gang frequented. Cops disguised me as a street-savvy ex-convict just released from prison. Willie took an interest in me right away. You might say I became his main squeeze.

"That six-year 'undercover affair' ended when Willie involved me in a drug heist in which he murdered the drivers. It was horrible. I managed to notify the police by leaving a note in a gas-station bathroom, and they finally rescued me at our motel hideout. Willie was about to kill me, too. It's a miracle I'm still alive." Lynn shook her head and sighed.

"There's a lot more to the story, of course," she continued. "One arrest led to another. Ultimately, there were more than thirty convictions, all a direct result of my testimony."

Pat's newspaper column publicized Lynn's remarkable story. Filmmaker John Kneubuhl read each installment. And he relied solely on Pat's articles to create a movie script called *The True Story of Lynn Stuart*. Pat's articles had provided the complete rough draft for Kneubuhl. The entire plot was there in the newspaper, and the movie maker bought it for just a dime a day.

The True Story of Lynn Stuart premiered in theaters on March 3, 1958. The weekend after its opening, Pat again approached George Chula at the Balboa Bay Club.

"How you doin' there, Georgie?" Pat said, grinning.

"Oh, hello Pat," said Chula, stirring his coffee. "I see you got your name on the big screen this week. Congratulations."

"Yeah, can you believe it? I accidently penned a movie script!"

"I hope KWIZ is paying you what you're worth. Maybe in the future you'll receive even larger rewards."

"Can't wait!" Pat gloated, feeling as if he had conquered the world. "Say, George, why don't you offer me a drink, buddy? After all, I treated last time!"

George fished in his pocket for some change.

*   *   *

Columbia Pictures released *The True Story of Lynn Stuart*, starring the legendary actress Betsy Palmer. Actor Jack Lord, later known for his role in the TV series *Hawaii Five-0*, was cast as Willie Down. This was Lord's first leading role in a major motion picture. Lending to the accuracy of the film, the real housewife behind Lynn Stuart served as technical adviser. Her face was kept covered while on the set. To further protect Lynn, Columbia Pictures stipulated that the film not be screened in California prisons where certain drug dealers might learn of her involvement in their arrests. One name in the title credits was not kept under wraps—Pat Michaels. Like Kneubuhl, Pat had also been handed a gift. His journalistic skills had now caught the attention of Hollywood. Pat was drawn to the fame as a moth is to a flame.

One night, standing in the grass outside his Santa Ana home, Pat looked up at the sky and thought of the small flashing light that had passed among the stars the previous year—the orbiting Russian Sputnik holding the infamous cosmonaut dog.

"Laika," he whispered, remembering the canine in space. "I'm so happy I think I could fly like you did!"

16
Divide and Conquer

Because Elsinore's council members were ethnically diverse, it was difficult for property owners to portray them as anti-Semitic. Realizing this, an attempt was made to whiten-up city hall. This required winning over council members of different ethnicities. The communist playbook offered a surefire "divide-and-conquer" strategy in such cases.

Needed first was some strong "for-the-people" messaging. Rhetoric is common in the world of politics and its use can be traced back to Marxist writings. Those who master political rhetoric insist that their side has everyone's best interest at heart, while painting the opposing party as the enemy. The major hurdle for property owners was convincing a few council members that they were on the wrong side morally and that they should switch to the side of the people.

"Our elected officials aren't looking out for the community," Morris declared at the Elsinore Property Owners Association meeting. "They're only watching their own backs."

"Right-o!" Slim shouted. "People need to know that we're the ones looking out for them."

"The average person on the street realizes this," Morris continued. "But the mayor and her cronies seem to be gaining the upper hand lately. We need to weaken them. I'm convinced that there might be a few among their ranks who are willing to defect and join us."

"Yes! Divide and conquer!" Slim shouted.

"Thank you, Slim. I appreciate your enthusiasm. As I've always said, however, we've got to be cagey and discreet about this."

"How do we show them they're on the wrong side of the issues?" James McGowan inquired.

"It's doubtful we'll convince the majority of the board," Morris conceded. "But there's a chance of persuading one or two. That's all we need. Then we wait to see if anyone else jumps ship."

Property owners agreed that the *Valley Times* would, once again, serve as the best vehicle for their newest strategy. A well-respected person would have to make the appeal, but who could that be?

"How about Frank Observer?" came a voice from the back of the room.

Morris thought for a moment. "Well, Frank's loyal to our cause, of course, but I don't think he has the for-the-people personality we need."

Indeed, the columnist's attacks against city officials were vicious. There was no way Frank could convince any of the officials to side with him or the residents. Plus, Observer's true communistic agenda was as plain as Stalin's was in 1941.

"How about James McGowan?" Slim suggested.

"How about someone the Senate isn't tailing?" Morris countered.

"Yeah, that narrows our options way down," Slim mumbled.

"There's always Sam," James chimed in.

Sam Kagan, sitting in the corner of the room, looked up when his name was mentioned. The homeowners began chattering to each other, and it was soon decided that Sam was ideal for the job. As a beloved camp director, no one would question his motives. He was an ordinary fellow with an ordinary job. He held no rank and had no red target on his back, as did Morris Kominsky and James McGowan. A background check would not even uncover a traffic violation. Because of his bashful disposition, few noticed him. His neighbors called him Silent Sam.

"What do you say, my friend?" Morris asked a few moments later.

There was a long pause, and everyone's eyes focused again on Sam.

"Okay. I guess I'll do it," Sam said quietly. "Tell me where I have to start."

Morris smiled and looked at all the attendees, sensing that the tide of public opinion was about to turn in their favor again. "Start with council member Chon Villa. He seems like easy pickings."

So Sam went to work. Townsfolk soon learned that Mr. Kagan was more timid in person than he was in print. On October 9, 1957, he wrote an open letter to the *Valley Times*, urging Chon Villa to desert his colleagues at once and join the Elsinore Property Owners Association. Silent

Sam shamelessly capitalized on Villa's Mexican heritage, stating: "All too often a member of a persecuted group, who achieves a little 'status,' falls for the blandishments of the very people who despise him, but are willing to use him."

Sam went as far as to include Councilman Villa's home phone number in his publication. He instructed readers, "Please phone him and encourage him to make a break and line up with the people."

Most who knew Sam were surprised by the aggressive and confrontational tone in his letters. But they still picked up their phones. The battle raged on in the dusty town of Elsinore.

17

King of L.A.

Never did Pat imagine his name being linked to the likes of a known mobster. Pat typically had no use for such scoundrels. Yet Pat stirred controversy on his radio broadcast by taking the side of a criminal who was currently making news. Pat managed to get on the wrong end of the law by publicly and proudly defending the notorious crime lord Meyer Harris "Mickey" Cohen.

After the assassination of mobster Bugsy Siegel in 1947, Mickey Cohen became known as the "King of Los Angeles." Not only had Mickey previously served as Bugsy's personal bodyguard, but he also became his right-hand lieutenant in financing some of the construction and initiating criminal operations at the Flamingo Hotel in Las Vegas. This joint venture included both West-Coast and East-Coast crime lords. At the Flamingo, Mickey ran the "sports book" operations and also oversaw the "race wire," which quickly grew into the national spinal cord for horse betting.

After Bugsy and his girlfriend were caught skimming money from the operation, East-Coast mobsters executed him in his Beverly Hills home. One of the nine gunshots hitting Bugsy blew out his left eyeball.

Infuriated, Mickey pursued the killers to the luxurious Hotel Roosevelt in Hollywood where he believed they were hiding. Mickey arrived with a pair of semiautomatic handguns. From the lobby entrance, he blasted shots everywhere. People fled as shards of ceiling tile and chandelier glass flew through the air along with chunks of the marble walls.

"Come out with your hands up, you East-Coast assassin scum!" Mickey screamed between shots. "If you know what's good for you, you'll meet me outside this hotel in ten minutes!"

Mickey strode out of the devastated hotel. A minute later he heard the sound of approaching police sirens, and he fled.

As muscle for the Jewish Mafia, Mickey maintained strong ties to both Italian and American Mafia leaders, such as his idol Al Capone. He was a short, pudgy man and his favorite foods were ice cream and pastries. Despite his ordinary appearance, word on the street was that no one should trifle with Mickey. He was a skilled fighter with a violent temper and enough wealth to buy off the entire Los Angeles Police Department. Indeed, he had many of the cops in his pocket, thus many of them turned a blind eye to his widespread racketeering.

The payoffs to the cops failed to make Mickey immune to danger, however. After several attempts on his life by rival West-Coast gangsters, notably Jack Dragna, Mickey converted his posh Brentwood mansion into a fortress stocked with an arsenal that would have defeated Mexico during the Battle of the Alamo.

Mickey's lucrative operations included gambling, narcotics, bootlegging, prostitution, and control of labor unions. A newspaper, a wire tapper, and some corrupt high-ranking authorities—including a state attorney general—helped him maintain his control over these crimes of vice. Many of L.A.'s top politicians bowed to Mickey, as did Hollywood stars such as Frank Sinatra, Dean Martin, and Sammy Davis Jr., according to some accounts. Those who didn't kowtow to Mickey were blackmailed.

Although local authorities looked the other way, the Feds kept a close watch. One agent was determined to take Mickey down. He was Federal Bureau of Narcotics Investigator, Howard Chappell. An eventual encounter between the two led to a fistfight, and Mickey was booked for assault. The charges didn't stick; a witness testified that Agent Chappell threw the first blow, so Mickey was acquitted.

Because of Mickey's notoriety, his arrest and subsequent trial became headline news on major media outlets. As often was the case, Pat Michaels drew his own conclusions about the events. Sympathetic to the underdog mobster, Pat announced on air that Mickey "has been framed." To make matters worse, Pat attacked Agent Chappell, insisting he was the one who should be indicted for assault. The next thing Pat knew, the law was after him, and he was promptly ordered to appear before a Federal Grand Jury.

The serving officers, Federal Agents Goodman and Read, demanded a copy of the news transcript. "If you hand it over, you can ignore the subpoena," Goodman told him. "I'm warning you, Michaels, you'll be saved a lot of headaches if you retract those incriminating remarks against Chappell on your next show!"

Pat was advised by counsel to obey the subpoena regardless of what Goodman told him. Two days later, Pat met with Chappell.

"The subpoena's just a formality to ensure that we receive a copy of the news transcript, Michaels. Again, there won't be any need to appear before the Grand Jury," Chappell told him. Nevertheless, Chappell refused to sign a waiver of appearance. Pat was suspicious. Something didn't smell right.

Pat finally did appear before the Grand Jury hearing. To his surprise, he was told, "Your testimony is not needed. And beyond that, the United States Attorney's Office knows nothing of the subpoena."

To be spared from future harassment, Pat reluctantly surrendered to his adversaries and announced his grudging retraction exactly one week after the initial broadcast.

Although Pat finally conceded to a more accurate version of the Cohen story, he was left embittered by the arrogance and foul play of Chappell. Pat filed charges in Superior Court for the County of Los Angeles. He claimed abuse of process, violation of constitutional rights, and illegal search and seizure.

His claim argued that all of the defendants "acted in excess of their authority" and that the subpoena was "not procured on behalf of the United States," but was "obtained and served by defendants for personal and ulterior purposes." He further purported that defendants "had no authority to obtain and/or serve said subpoena," and it was not "obtained or served by defendants for any purpose or proceeding then pending or sought to be pending before the Federal Grand Jury."*

In addition to criminal charges, Pat included a demand for $10,500 for emotional damages. Ultimately, the case was dismissed. Pat did not relent though, and he filed for an appeal. This was also dismissed because he didn't submit it within the allotted thirty days.

Pat didn't feel defeated by this ordeal. If anything, it became wind beneath his wings, and he fancied himself a spokesman in the battle for truth and justice. By this time, his popular broadcast had earned him recognition as one of Southern California's most noteworthy and controversial reporters. Even his retractions were sensational.

Like Mickey Cohen, Pat made as many friends in high places as he did enemies. This suited him just fine. He needed enemies. News reporting was dull without them.

_____

* *Patrick Michaels v. Howard W. Chappell et al. United States Court of Appeals Ninth Circuit (15 June 1960).*

18

Fluoride Hoax

With the press serving as a bloody battlefront, the water war in Elsinore raged on. In his weekly *Valley Times* column, called "Elsinore's Fluoride Hoax," Sam Farber pulled out the big guns, taking shots at the State Department of Health. In an open letter to its director, Dr. Malcolm Merrill, Farber insisted that the department was mistaken concerning the potential dangers of Elsinore's mineral water. There were no reports of anyone harmed by it, nor did any conclusive research exist describing the possible associated risks. Farber further asserted that the city water system carried higher fluoride levels than local water. In closing, Farber pointed fingers at City Attorney Arthur Littleworth, the City Council, and the *Elsinore City Sun*, alleging that they were all part of a coordinated hoax and were the willing pawns of the State Department of Health.

Frank Observer also continued to breathe fire, threatening a libel suit against any "witch hunters" who dared label him as a Communist instigator. As it turned out, this ultimatum was the last missile he blasted from the *Valley Times*. With his newspaper constantly besmirched by mudslinging, the editor finally grew tired and stopped printing Frank Observer's angry rants.

Property owners also lightened up on the name-calling, but they did manage to publish one final piece in the *Valley Times*. The paper stated, "Regardless of what scare stories they [the City Council] may attempt to peddle, the basic ideas remain: clean water, clean government, and harmonious relations amongst all our people!"

With his popular "Elsinore's Fluoride Hoax" column approaching its imminent end, even Sam Farber softened. His final article simply stated, "[this is something] we intended to spring as a surprise in court, but which we are now going to tell to a higher court—the people of Elsinore." Although Sam still favored the idea of overhauling City Hall, he did have second thoughts about the potential dangers of fluoride. If by chance it was harmful, he didn't want that on his conscience. His farewell article suggested ideas for treating mineral water. He also called for an investigation to make it safe. Sam's last word on the subject was a plea to end "all the silly wrangling and squabbling."

Although the roiling public dispute was reduced to a simmer, SUAC investigators continued their probe. Their report concluded: "There is no question about the supply of mineral water being the chief factor behind Elsinore's economic stability. When the supply was shut off, protests were only natural. The real problem consisted of the fact that at least two of the leaders of the embattled Property Owners Association had long Communist records, and that there were many Communist sympathizers and fellow travelers who resided in the community. Furthermore, the campaign of relentless vituperation against the incumbent city administration effectively undermined public confidence..."

This widespread suspicion and disfavor affected every city official. The Chief of Police and the City Attorney were especially wounded in the crossfire. With elections around the corner, the outlook for reelection and resolution grew only gloomier. The POA's propaganda campaign, as ugly and unfair as it was, had succeeded. City seats were up for grabs, and dissident property owners were rabid to grab the reins of power from the indurate elected elites.

19

Sentenced to Die

Surrounded by the aroma of cigarette smoke and bacon, Pat sat at the kitchen table with a coffee cup in one hand and a burning Kent in the other. As usual, the *Orange County Register* was fanned out in front of him like a roadmap. Even the tempting smell of breakfast didn't cause his eyes to leave the headlines. He always insisted on a hot breakfast with his paper, but it was generally cold before he noticed it; he customarily devoured the news first.

Lois slipped into the kitchen chair beside him and leaned near, quietly reading with him the story on page one.

Pat glanced at her briefly and then looked back at the news. The silent smoke curled upward.

"It's hard to believe someone so young was capable of such a crime," he finally muttered, shaking his head.

"It's tragic," Lois agreed. "He took a life back in 1952. Now he's finally going to pay for it with his own."

"So young," Pat repeated. "The killer was only eighteen when he did it. I don't know how I feel about that."

"Cases like these do make one wonder," Lois conceded. "But I still feel more sorry for that poor girl's mother than I do for the murderer."

There was no debating Billy Rupp's guilt in this first-degree murder case. The Yorba Linda youth had confessed to everything when he was initially arrested for the crime five years previously. Yes, it was Billy who broke into his neighbor's peaceful home where fifteen-year-old babysitter Ruby Ann Payne was caring for three small children. With no discernable motive, the crazed intruder clobbered the defenseless girl over the head with a hammer and then shot her twice with a .22 when she tried to escape. He was cutting the clothes off her lifeless body when the oldest child entered the room. That's when Billy panicked, grabbed his rifle, and ran out the door like a roach in the light.

Days later, after subsisting in his hideout on a diet of pretzels, he was found dining at a cafe in the neighboring city of Brea.

The horrific nature of Billy's crime included an automatic death penalty. This created a moral dilemma for the jurors who heard his case in 1952. The options were either to find Billy not guilty, thus allowing a confessed killer to go free, or to declare him guilty, which would send him to the gas chamber.

The jurors who heard the case of The People v. William Francis Rupp were not informed of Billy's complete medical history dating back to his adolescence. He had been institutionalized when he was fourteen after brutally assaulting another female. Psychiatrists in that case had no difficulty in diagnosing Billy as "schizophrenic, mentally deranged, and dangerous." This expert opinion kept Billy locked away in a mental hospital until he reached adulthood. Because Billy was a juvenile at the time of his first crime, these records were declared inadmissible at his trial for the Ruby Payne murder. Therefore, he was pronounced sane at the time of the Payne killing, and he was found guilty as charged.

After the death penalty was pronounced, Billy's sister wrote to the California state governor to plead for his life. Her letter offered a graphic account of Billy's tormented childhood. It also put his appointment with the San Quentin gas chamber on hold for several years. His sister's appeal substantiated the psychiatric findings, but it could not prevent the inevitable. Billy still had to die.

Then Attorney George Chula came on the scene, and he featured himself as the perfect defense lawyer for Billy. He was not willing to accept such a harsh verdict against the troubled teen—but his moralism did not stem from altruism or idealism. As usual, George was motivated by notoriety, power, and money.

George's strategy for defending the hapless Billy was to garner public sympathy and letters of support for overturning the unfair death sentence. His ultimate aim was to coax the jurors who had condemned Billy to provide testimonials informing the court that they had subsequently changed their minds. The big challenge was locating all twelve jurors after five years had passed, and he only had a few days to do it before the hearing began. Hoping for a lightning-quick miracle and a favor from a friend, George wasted no time in calling KWIZ.

"Good morning, Pat. You're just the man I want to speak to!"

"Oh really? What do you need, George?"

"Pat, buddy. I think we're really going to be able to help each other out on this one," George said. He paused, hoping to arouse the reporter instinct in Pat. "Just like we did together on the Lynn Stuart story."

"Well, George, if I recall correctly, I don't think you actually gave me very much info on the Stuart story. I mean, after all was said and done... Nevertheless, I'm listening."

"Seriously, Pat, this is a matter of life and death. And I can definitely promise you a good story. But time is of the essence."

"Okay, George. Shoot."

"It has to do with Billy Rupp."

"The murderer?"

"Yes. My task is to get him off death row."

"Tell me more," said Pat. In the next few minutes, George filled him in on the details of the case and the impending appeal in court.

As Pat learned more about the case, the skepticism natural to his vocation subsided and his interest grew. He realized that working again with George could propel him toward even further broadcasting success. Trying to control his rising enthusiasm, he nodded and said, "Yes, George, I see your point. Count me in!"

The Rupp case would have excited any news-hungry reporter. This story was of more than local interest. It was national headline material. There was crime, suspense, mystery, drama, and controversy on every level—ethical, moral, and political. In addition, George was tackling something never attempted before, a move undocumented in any law book—using the very jurors who sentenced a criminal to die to defend that same criminal's right to life.

Pat included Billy Rupp's story in all his subsequent newscasts. At the top of every hour Pat Michaels campaigned for compassion, announcing the horrific story of poor Billy Rupp. He recited the details of Billy's tragic upbringing and fragile mental condition. Although these broadcasts drew great sympathy from the community at large, the bigger purpose was to reach the ears of those jurors who had judged Billy guilty. So, with each hourly report, Pat urged all twelve jurors to come forward and contact George Chula immediately. As a testimony to the widespread influence of Pat's broadcasts in Southern California, most of the jurors responded.

George communicated with all the jurors who had contacted him, and he asked them to sign an affidavit stating: "I would not have voted for the death penalty had it been known to me that there was a method whereby William Francis Rupp could be incarcerated for life without possibility of parole."

Signing the affidavits required little convincing. Jurors signed readily. Among the first was Mrs. Lucille Lanford of Santa Ana. At the original hearing, she had held out against a death verdict for more than twenty-eight hours before giving in to "fatigue and other pressures."

"At the time," she told Chula, "I believed that in certain cases the death penalty was all right. With Rupp, our choice was either to kill him or leave it to chance that he might be turned free again in the future. But now, this whole case has me so mixed up, I don't think I even believe in capital punishment anymore."

Despite the jurors' change of heart, the signed affidavits failed to sway California Governor Goodwin Knight. On November 7, 1958, Billy Rupp ate a hearty meal that included French fries, doughnuts, chocolate milk, ice cream, and a salad. Then he walked to the gas chamber and died.

The attempt to save Billy had failed, but the joint collaboration of Reporter Pat Michaels and Attorney George Chula solidified a deep bond between the two.

"I owe you one," George vowed to Pat, shaking his hand. Indeed, this debt was not forgotten. The two men would meet again in Elsinore.

* * *

The Billy Rupp case, along with the efforts of Chula and Michaels to save him, were reported in the Los Angeles Times on August 30, 1957. Three decades later the story was featured as a special interest column in the Orange Coast Magazine Oct. 1987, page 94

The Ten Commandments above Elsinore's synagogue.
Damage is visible above tablet 2.

The Crescent Bath House

Not everyone took the fluoride scare seriously

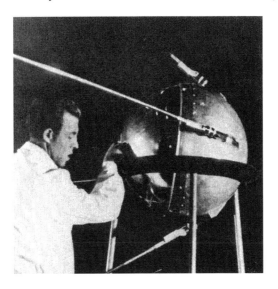

Sputnik 1 – The Mouse That Roared

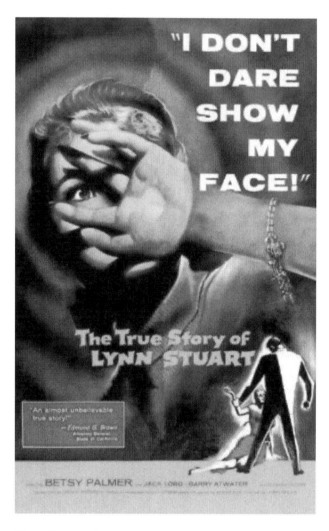

The True Story of Lynn Stuart. Based on news articles by Pat Michaels.

QUITE SUBDUED —Mickey Cohen, bearing black
eye, is taken up in County Jail to change clothes
before appearing at U.S. Commissioner's hearing.
Times photo

Mickey Cohen Facing
U.S. Assault Charge

Pat Michaels finds himself entangled in a legal battle after
accusing a federal agent of assaulting Mobster Mickey Cohen

CONFESSED SLAYER — William Rupp, right, being led into Orange County Jail by Deputy Sheriff Oliver McCarter, after his capture in Brea cafe, and shortly before he confessed slaying Ruby Ann Payne last Friday in Yorba Linda home where she was working as baby sitter. Scores of Southland officers had searched for him five days.

Convicted murderer Billy Rupp gets the death sentence.
The efforts of Pat Michaels failed to save him

Pat Michaels with KTLA news team.

BEGINNING TONITE!

The 10 o'clock news is on channel 5

Clete Roberts   Tom Harmon   Pat Michaels

See the BIG  FINAL

10:00 to 10:30 MONDAY-FRIDAY

The only complete round-up of world and local news, sports, and news analysis!

Watch the Pace Setting Telecopter-News Station

KTLA

Channel 5 Los Angeles

Pat Michaels narrates for "The Atomic Submarine"

Pat Michaels and family
(Pat, Lois, Rick, Karen, Terrance & Kathy)

Pat Michaels on location in Elsinore

Interview with Communist James McGowan

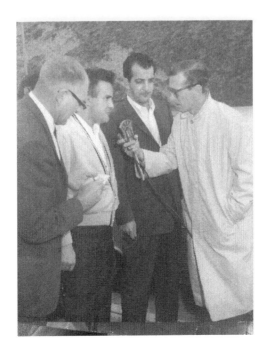

Interview with Elsinore city officials

Continued on Page 9-A ism.

CALCULATED CAMPAIGN LAUNCHED

Jews of California Resort Hit by Wave of Terrorism

LOS ANGELES—(JTA)—The KTLA television station here has aired an hour-long documentary program asserting that a nearby resort city, Elsinore, was on the verge of violence against its Jewish citizens. Officials of the station said that to get the report, Pat Michaels and other members of the station's news staff were sworn in as members of Elsinore's police force "for their own safety."

A KTLA special news release, announcing the "City of Hate" program, declared that the news staff had "uncovered a situation which parallels the nightmare of Nazi Germany with frightening fidelity." It stressed that "the terrorism is part of a calculated campaign designed to drive out the large Jewish population which has gathered in the resort city." The documentary was shown twice.

The program showed that damage had been done to synagogues and centers in Elsinore, which is 72 miles southeast of Los Angeles. The news staff interviewed officials and residents of Elsinore to determine their reactions to widening signs of anti-Semitism. These included threatening letters, paint bombings, and stonings. The program charged that a concealed organization, calling itself the International Freedom Fighters, was responsible.

Originally, Elsinore's tourist

Continued on Page 9-A

Clip from the Jewish Telegraph Agency

California District Attorney Stanley Mosk

Corp. of America, Lanolin Plus Division, Newark, N. J., reassigned Rybutol vitamin account from D & C to Cohen & Aleshire, N. Y., and awarded Daniel & Charles campaign for "major new product," to be launched in radio and tv June 1. Cohen & Aleshire plans extensive tv, radio and print campaign for Rybutol.

Slander charge dismissed in 'City of Hate' tv case

Indictments charging slander among other things against former Los Angeles tv announcer Pat Michaels and others were dismissed March 31 by Indio, Calif., Superior Court Judge Merrill Brown, who said indictments were too vague as to who was slandered and how.

Defamation charges were made by mayor or nearby Elsinore, Calif., and others after 1959 telecast of "City of Hate," presented by Mr. Michaels on KTLA (TV), on alleged anti-Semitism in Elsinore. Mr. Michaels is now with KABC Los Angeles.

Ch.4 bid dropout allowed

FCC Chief Hearing Examiner James D. Cunningham Friday granted request of Rocky Mountain Tele Stations to dismiss its application for ch. 4 at Reno, Nev., dismissing with prejudice. Remaining applicant is Circle L Inc.

Weisberg to Trans-Lux Tv

Robert Weisberg, well-known to tv station executives throughout country in his post as executive in charge of buying films for Tv Stations Inc. for more than five years, is resigning that position shortly to join Trans-Lux Television Corp., New York, in newly-created post. Details of new job, said to be unique in industry, will be announced in early May but it probably will concern itself with servicing of tv programs to stations.

A surprise decision: charges are dismissed

20

Casualties of War

"I've always considered it a high honor to serve this community," Cheryl announced before a row of somber faces at the city council gathering. "But I cannot continue under this ever-expanding cloud of doubt. The citizens of Elsinore have lost confidence in me. It would be unfair to remain as mayor without their trust."

"If you resign, those commies win!" Jose Torres protested. "We can't let that happen."

"I have no fight left in me, councilman. Besides, it's my family that's paying the highest price. They're my first priority."

Not only had Cheryl French become the first woman to serve as mayor of Elsinore, she was first to ever resign from the position. Although she had conducted herself ethically, legally, and properly, the propaganda madness was injurious, causing widespread distrust in her ability to govern.

In French's defense, her hands were tied. Property owners demanded what she could never deliver. The State Department of Health had declared the mineral water toxic, and the order to shut it off came directly from them. Mayor French's only crime was in obeying the higher authority. Unfortunately for Cheryl, property owners didn't see it that way. Instead, they saw her as falling in line with "Jew-hating bureaucrats." "She's a willing pawn," Morris insisted, "and a co-conspirator in the fluoride scare!"

As unfounded as the allegations were, they served their intended purpose in creating a climate of contempt and confusion, thus forcing Mayor French out of office. With barely a few months left in her term, she surrendered her seat. Never in the history of Elsinore had a city official endured such vicious attacks. The ordeal exhausted her physically and wounded her emotionally. Despite it all, Cheryl French bowed out with her integrity in tow, arguably leaving a legacy of higher honor than the vile Communists who stood against her.

"What will we do without Cheryl?" Torres asked.

"We'll tuck our heads between our legs and kiss our sorry tails goodbye," replied Councilman Bobbitt. "It's over for us, too."

Bobbitt's negative prediction was prophetic. After Cheryl's resignation, Elsinore's remaining city officials fell like dominos. By election time, each and every one had been removed from office and replaced, including the Chief of Police, the City Attorney, and other key leaders. Members of the Property Owners Association readily filled those vacancies. Their objective to control local government was finally in their grasp.

Having gained recognition for his column in the *San Jacinto Valley Times*, Sam Farber easily won his place on city council. Sam Kagan was also appointed to an open seat. His efforts to entice former council member Chon Villa to leave the "corruption and prejudice" of city government had earned him a loyal following. Many saw this unassuming camp director as a modern-day Robin Hood who would gladly fight for the commoners.

The real hero of the election was Thomas Yarborough. It was the popular evangelist Aimee Semple McPherson who had brought him to Elsinore years earlier. As a firm believer in the healing properties of mineral water, McPherson built an elaborate mansion on the shores overlooking the spring lake. She hired Yarborough as the maintenance man, and she paid him well. In time, Yarborough was able to open an upholstery shop downtown. His thriving business allowed him to invest in real estate.

Yarborough had previously served on city council from 1948 to 1956, making him a shoo-in for reappointment during the water-war election of 1958. Of the many involved in the Elsinore controversy, Yarborough stood out as a voice of reason. His sole desire was to serve the community that had contributed to his success. But opportunists had invaded city council now, and Thomas was outnumbered.

21
The Big Three

Closing papers were signed as quickly as they were produced. It was the ultimate dream home: a luxurious two-story, four-bedroom edifice in the affluent hills of Sherman Oaks. Lois was just glad there wasn't a swimming pool in the yard, unlike at their previous Santa Ana residence. At the old house, two-year-old Terrance had wandered out the back door one afternoon and subsequently fell into the deep end. He would have drowned had his sister not noticed him floating there.

At the new property, Pat was more interested in the detached office space. He liked to think of it as the perfect hideaway. He could write without interruption there, away from the children's din and the other annoyances of family life. He craved the solitude, and it drew him toward this piece of real estate even though the mortgage was more than he could afford. "The new job requires I produce at a furious rate, which justifies this upgrade," he told Lois.

Lois liked the new house well enough, but—as usually was the case with her flamboyant and impulsive husband—she silently worried about the future.

"Didn't I tell you doors would swing open?" George Chula reminded Pat at the Bay Club. "Never would've happened had I not given you that lead on Lynn Stuart."

"As I mentioned before, George, it wasn't much of a lead," Pat replied, tossing down his martini.

"It was enough, Pat. You wouldn't have had a story without it."

"You win, George. Let's celebrate. Next round is on me."

"To the next Edward R. Murrow!" George raised his glass. "By the way, I never did see my name in the closing credits of that movie."

"It was squeezed in small print between Jack Lord's and Betsy Palmer's," Pat laughed.

"Yeah, very small print," responded George.

When KTLA called, Pat didn't hesitate for a minute. It was the opportunity of a lifetime, working in television for a major market—the greater Los Angeles area and beyond! But the station's wide reach was just the icing on the cake. Pat would be joining forces with veteran broadcaster and fellow war correspondent Clete Roberts.

KTLA management had bargained hard after Clete. They snatched him from KNXT, the local CBS affiliate, offering him an all-or-nothing proposition and a salary that surpassed any in the industry. Clete accepted the position and brought his team of cameramen to KTLA with him.

Through his own company, U.S. Television News, Clete deployed cameramen across the globe, predominantly in known hotspots where stories exploded like grenades.

Never was there a reporter as innovative as Clete Roberts. No other possessed an international network such as he had developed while working at KTLA. As lead anchorman, he single-handedly revolutionized television news. Camera crews from foreign fields sent film showing breaking stories while Clete reported from the local newsroom. This arrangement was never attempted before, and as a result, KTLA took the number-one spot in the TV Nielson ratings.

Also joining the ranks on Clete's team was football "Hall of Famer" and Heisman Trophy winner Tom Harmon. Harmon, who announced the sports segment, was among the first of pro athletes to transition from the playing field to a spot in front of the camera. Harmon had been a number-one pick by the Los Angeles Rams, but his stint in pro ball was short lived. Leg injuries suffered in World War II eventually took him off the field. Harmon was not taken out of the game completely though. Millions of fans in Southern California listened daily to his expert sports commentary.

The dynamic broadcasting trio of Roberts, Michaels, and Harmon quickly became known as television's "Big Three" in the state. Clete covered breaking international stories, and Pat handled the local front. And there was no shortage of local stories in the ever-growing metropolis of Los Angeles and surrounding counties. The bigger challenge for Pat was discerning the events that deserved his attention. After making those decisions, the crew eagerly supported him. Clete even assigned several cameramen to Pat.

All three individuals were celebrities in the world of broadcast journalism. Although Pat and Clete were both recognizable figures, they also bore an uncanny resemblance to one another. Pat's own children teased him about the similarities. The colleagues were almost identical in build and coloring, and they both groomed their hair and mustaches in the tradition of movie star Clark Gable. Also, they each dressed in loose dark suits with matching ties. Adding to the confusion, both men spoke with the typical broadcaster's deep bravado. To the casual observer, the only distinguishing feature between the two was the Clark Kent glasses Pat wore.

The two mirrored one another externally, but they were polar opposites inside. Each approached his craft differently: Clete was a purist and Pat a sensationalist. Clete painted stories by the number, whereas Pat viewed each news story as an incomplete canvas that could benefit from the creative brushstrokes of a master newscaster.

Most journalists in the 1950s realized that their word was nearly sacred, regardless of its veracity. "A story doesn't have to be believable to be believed," was the popular credo of many reporters. "Only the messenger needs to be believed, and the reporter's press card takes care of that minor detail! Call a man a lawyer and the public is suspicious. Call him a reporter and people think he descended from Honest Abe Lincoln!"

Most reporters of the day lived up to the people's trust, but some took advantage of it as they clawed their way up the ladder of success.

The head producer at KTLA likened news reporting to canned food at the grocery store. "The true story's on the back of the can: ingredients, nutritional facts, location of the manufacturer. There is no intent to impress, just to report. The front of the can is more appealing. Its job is to attract and advertise. The language and pictures on the front are colorful and bigger than life. Marketers and designers can present the product as better than it is.

"Some reporters are like the back of a can," the producer continued, "and others are more like the front. Different reporters handle the same job differently."

In the case of Clete and Pat, the contrast was clear.

Clete was the can's back label: detailed, factual, serious, researched, truthful, reliable.

Pat was the front: colorful, splashy, larger than life, prone to exaggeration. And sometimes inclined toward fabrication.

22

Fatal Shot

The election results in Elsinore prompted raised eyebrows among SUAC investigators. As noted in the 1959 SUAC report: "Former members of the Elsinore Police Department have stated that the residents of that city 'had the wool pulled over their eyes by Communist agitators who had been moving into the city for the last three years.'"

The report went on to say, "The records of this Committee disclosed that at least thirty-five of the most active agitators and propagandists, who participated in the effort to get control of the city government of Elsinore, have long and persistent records of Communist-front affiliation and similar agitation in other localities. Many of the voters in the municipal election, that resulted in the ouster of the old officials and their replacement with new ones backed by the Property Owners Association, had moved into Elsinore—despite rumors of political and economic disaster in that city—from Los Angeles, just in time to be eligible to vote in the election."

Despite the successful placement of property owners on the city board, the administration at the Elsinore Valley Municipal Water District didn't change. The members of this board were not elected officials, although they did answer directly to the elected California Department of Health. Because of this, the property owners of Elsinore could not yet declare complete victory in their war for water. The city election had created a new battlefront, and the powerful antagonists occupying Elsinore's city seats began attacking the EVMWD.

The newly elected council wasted no time in flexing its municipal muscle, unanimously agreeing to restore 100% distribution of the mineral water. EVWMD board members refused to cooperate, however, choosing instead to abide by the state's mandate. As a result, the POA and city council now focused their smear tactics on members of the EVMWD. The pressure ultimately led to the resignation of the department's founding president, Everett L. Grubb, who also served on the board of the California Water Plan.

Even after Grubb's departure, the EVWMD did not allow Elsinore's mineral water to flow, still asserting that it was unsafe for consumption. By this time, studies on children's teeth supported the idea that fluoride was potentially harmful. This research did little to convince those citizens who swore that the natural spring water had healing properties. One such believer was Slim Wiggins, who burst into an EVWMD board meeting one evening.

As he read aloud the meeting agenda that night, Superintendent Clark Ramsey was startled as the rear door of the conference room flung open so violently that it bounced off the adjacent wall. In shocked surprise, Clark saw Slim Wiggins striding toward him.

Ramsey moved back in his chair, recognizing how agitated Wiggins was. Ramsey was well aware of the rancher's history of angry outbursts and instability. The superintendent's mouth became dry. "Slim?" was all he could say.

Slim glared through narrowed eyes at Clark. All the board members gasped when Slim pulled a pistol from under his shirt and aimed it at the superintendent's head.

Ramsey swallowed hard and his hands shook. "Slim," he uttered hoarsely. "Slim. Please. Put that thing away. You can't solve anything like this…"

"Nothing ever gets solved by the likes of you, Clark," Slim snarled.

"Slim, think about what you're doing!" Ramsey cried.

"The way I see it, the only thing in this city that stands in the way of our water and livelihood is you! I'm tired of waiting for you smooth-talking hypocrites to do something for the people instead of for yourselves. And I'm going to fix that, once and for all!"

"Slim, Slim, listen! You're not seeing the whole picture," Ramsey said, gripping the armrests of his chair.

"Don't even move a hair, Clark. I'm giving you a choice. Say we can have our water back, or start saying your dang prayers! You got five seconds to decide!"

"It's not up to me, Slim."

"That, Mr. Ramsey, was the wrong thing to say…"

Board members screamed at the gun's report. The bullet hit Clark between the eyes, killing him instantly. Slim then turned and shot again, seriously wounding another board member who was reaching for his holster.

In the smoke, noise, and confusion, most of the others escaped through a nearby window. Slim stood silently, looking down at the blood on Clark's face and hearing the moans of the other man. Slim's arms hung limp at his sides.

The secretary of the board was hidden behind a chair. He was a large man, skilled in self-defense. He suddenly jumped up and tackled Slim from behind, throwing him to the floor and pinning him under the weight of his body. A smack to the head stunned Slim, and the secretary was able to hold the murderer until the police arrived several minutes later.

As the officers tried to apply the cuffs, Slim again became violent, trying to resist arrest. "I did what was right!" he screamed. "I did it for the people! The people! You need to understand!"

Slim's shirt was torn during his fight with the cops. On his chest was a tattoo of a hammer and sickle.

The officers finally subdued Slim and dragged him to their cruiser outside. "It doesn't end here!" Slim yelled as frightened neighbors watched from their windows. "There are more of us than you realize!"

The murder created enough fear in the EVWMD to weaken its resolve against community pressure. Representatives were now too afraid to fight back. Property owner Carl Kegley, as newly elected City Attorney, took full advantage of this fact and demanded a full and immediate restoration of Elsinore's natural water.

"Our demands have also been made known at the state level," Carl asserted. "The Department of Health is now in complete agreement. As of today, tap water is to be shut off, and mineral water is to be released at full volume."

News traveled fast, finally reaching the jailhouse. "We won, Slim!" Morris told him. "We got our water back at last!"

"Really?" asked Slim.

"Yes, comrade," Morris continued. "I know you're in jail—a tough place—but think about what you accomplished for the cause! You performed ideally. You're putting the common good above your own welfare. It's the people's cause! Power to the people! Sacrifices had to be made. Remember, brother, we're at war! You are a hero!"

Slim rolled over on his bunk toward the wall.

23

Bon Michelle

Working in the television industry opened doors of opportunity beyond Pat's wildest imagination. Once again, Hollywood took notice of him. His baritone voice was perfect as narrator for the sci-fi movie *The Atomic Submarine*. This undersea thriller was about a naval submarine crew investigating mysterious disappearances of merchant ships traveling across the North Pole. Under the ice was an alien craft so evil it would make Lake Elsinore's sea serpent flee in terror.

The eerie film was hardly a major blockbuster, although *The Atomic Submarine* did gain attention as a cult classic on the small screen, at least for those who enjoyed campy B movies. The acting and directing were subpar, and the low-budget effects elicited more chuckles than shivers from its audience. Nevertheless, Pat's experience as narrator looked impressive on his resume.

Pat was now living his fantasy, shining among the stars of Sherman Oaks Hills, where the lights of Hollywood could be seen from Mulholland Drive. Money started flowing into his life like rain after a drought. His suits now included designer labels, and he began wearing a solid-gold Saint Christopher medal on a chain around his neck. His daughters were bused to a private Christian school.

"Lois," he said after work one day. "We're buying a yacht! I'm getting a great deal on a brand new cabin cruiser!"

"What?" cried Lois. "Pat, I know we have some money now, and some people think we're rich. But a yacht? Yachts are expensive! Why do we need a yacht?"

"For fun!" Pat responded. "And for show! I've been poor for too long, and I want to show people that I finally made it big!" Pat left the room to find a pack of cigarettes. Lois stood alone and dumbfounded at this latest surprise announcement from her spontaneous husband.

Photographers were present the day Pat and Lois christened the bow of their new vessel, the *Bon Michelle*. Lois bit her lower lip as she attempted to smile for the camera. Pat was unconcerned about the craft's expense, whereas Lois found herself worrying even about the cost of the fine champagne they had just lost in the sea. Lois continued smiling bravely, however, saying nothing.

With Pat's success came VIP status at the prestigious Balboa Bay Club, which provided another convenient place for Pat to escape the boring routines of life. Family vacations began at the club, where Lois and the four kids would assemble with their bags in anticipation of cruising through the blue waves toward the beautiful Catalina Island, southwest of Los Angeles. The Michaels family customarily endured choppy waters, usually causing all four children to grow seasick.

When the boat returned to the mainland, a happy host of socialites were there to revive the pale-green kids with Shirley Temples, whereas Dad and Mom sipped Bloody Marys from crystal stemware.

"This is a great club, right Lois?" Pat said, happily reclining in his poolside lounge chair.

"Well, Pat," said Lois hesitantly, looking at him through her stylish new sunglasses. "I have to admit it. I do enjoy the relaxation."

"Yeah, I knew you'd like it babe," replied Pat, his eyes roving across the patio behind his own expensive pair of shades.

Pat's memories of his bleak childhood in the orphanage faded with every round of drinks he bought for his buddies at the harbor-side "Anchors and Oceans" bar. Suddenly everyone was his friend.

Filmmakers and club members were not the only ones to notice Pat's success. "That Pat Michaels is one cool cat," women at his workplace would say. With his wealth and charm, more than a few women flirted with him, even though they knew he had a wife and four children at home.

Pat held out as long as he could, but his beautiful and persistent young secretary finally wore down his defenses. "Come on, let's run out and grab some lunch," Pat would say with a smile. She always agreed. Then, later, they started having dinner together after work, which eventually led to his stopping by her apartment for a nightcap...

Lois was perturbed that Pat's job was taking more and more of his family time. I guess this is the price people pay for the good life, she told herself. But as she sat at the kitchen table night after night, helping restless kids with long division, she wondered whether there was something more to the good life than this.

124

Pat and his secretary saw more and more of each other. Soon Pat and his blonde companion were enjoying outings on the *Bon Michelle*, while Lois and the children stayed home.

Pat's private affair would have made sensational tabloid news, but Pat hoped this part of his life would never reach the headlines. He presented himself to the world as a churchgoing family man driven by deep religious convictions. Privately, his lust led him to yield to the most unsavory temptations. His duplicity demanded one cover-up after the next.

True to his character, Pat was living for the moment, ignoring potential negative consequences. But his lies and alibis became an ever-tightening web around him.

Despite his internal conflicts, Pat's external demeanor was carefree and confident. After all, he thought, trying to rationalize his behavior, *I've spent my whole life following my passions, and it's already led me to the pinnacle of success! Why should I stop now?*

Maintaining both his family and his playboy life was increasingly difficult. He felt torn. He loved his family, but he also loved his fling. He thrived on the ritual of religion as much as on the excitement of the rendezvous. He sought privacy, but he also sought publicity. He craved safety as much as danger.

Attempting to protect both worlds, he feared losing one, the other, or both. He couldn't decide between holiness and hedonism. His personal dilemma finally exploded into the biggest news story of his life. And it was also the saddest.

24
Grand Jury Report

After the mineral water was released, Riverside County officials empaneled a grand jury to investigate the allegations and accusations surrounding the Elsinore affair. Jury members received the task of evaluating evidence and naming those involved in malfeasance. All fingers pointed toward the newly elected city officials. Mayor Thomas Bartlett and the entire city council were indicted for conspiracy and for violating a state mandate prohibiting the distribution of untreated spring water.

It was the opinion of the grand jury that "They feloniously and knowingly conspired to willfully and unlawfully violate the terms and provisions of a water permit issued by the State Department of Public Health of the State of California, said permit issued in accordance with the provisions of the Health and Safety Code" (People v. Bartlett 199 Cal. App. 2d 173).

As the recognized ringleader of the uprising, Morris felt guilty about the indictment of so many of his cohorts. Not only did Morris mastermind the plot to control local government, he also led the campaign to restore the local water. Morris managed to dodge the bullet of blame in this case, but almost everyone else he encouraged and promoted for office took hits. Morris's sense of honor and justice was violated, and survivor guilt plagued his conscience.

The evening after the indictments were announced, Morris sat alone in his car and thought, I simply cannot allow my loyal comrades to pay the price for a war I waged. Besides, our town's precious water is at risk again, and I'm not about to sacrifice that either!

As the sun descended, he looked around at the streets of Elsinore. A new plan was slowly forming in his mind. Finally he shouted with raised fist, "The war continues!"

Morris wasted no time in calling a meeting with key officials, including the newly elected mayor, the police chief, and the city attorney.

"We need to crank up the propaganda machine again," Morris challenged. "The anti-Semitism campaign was effective in taking down our intended targets. Now we must go even further!"

All those in attendance agreed.

"Certainly a case could be made that the State Department of Health intended to drive Jews out of Elsinore," Morris continued.

City Attorney Kegley raised his hand and said, "Morris, don't forget that we have to be able to back up those allegations."

"It's as plain as day," Morris barked back. "They had our water shut off just to close down businesses, all which happen to be Jewish owned!"

Statistics shockingly supported Kominsky's allegations. It was Jewish business owners who were most affected by the mandate to cut off the mineral springs. And it was mainly Jewish citizens who were fleeing, broke and penniless, from Elsinore. With such undeniable data, "coincidence" would be a difficult defense even for a reputable state agency.

"How do we proceed?" asked Mayor Bartlett. "Frank Observer no longer holds the respect he once did. People think of him as a loose cannon. He's lost all credibility."

With a dismissive shake of his head, Morris squelched the notion of another "Mom-and-Pop" newspaper campaign. "Think higher!" he challenged.

It was obvious that attacking the state would require more than a small-town rag with limited distribution. "What about the *Los Angeles Times*?" Chief Bittle suggested.

"I'm leaning more toward television," Morris mused. He looked around the room with narrowed eyes, a smile playing at the corners of his mouth. "And I think I know just the man to call!"

Meanwhile in nearby Los Angeles, Pat Michaels was laughing and quaffing a martini with his secretary, Rhonda.

25

Dual Nature

"Lois," Pat told his wife. "Work is killing me. They want me to spend more and more time on location covering the news. It's grueling. I have to go all over the place!"

In truth, during the times he claimed he was working Pat was often staring into the eyes of his lady friend. His relationship with Rhonda had quickly developed into a full-blown affair. As a well-known personage, however, Pat couldn't appear just anywhere with a woman who wasn't his wife. So he frequently drove to the *Balboa Bay Club* alone, where he'd ship out by himself in the *Bon Michelle*. "I have to get away and clear my mind," he'd say to the dockworkers. He'd then land at a discrete port where his secret friend would climb aboard. Together they'd sail away into the Pacific.

Pat inevitably steered south toward Mexico, where even the best rabbit-ear antennas couldn't pick up KTLA's "Big Three News" broadcast. One popular stop on the way, however, was a nudist colony on the coast. Here Pat invited sun worshipers to climb aboard the *Bon Michelle*. The upper deck, where Pat had entertained his children, became a scene of lewdness and debauchery.

Pat laughingly encouraged the colony members to embark on the pleasure cruise, but his hospitality was not principally motivated by lust. For Pat, these unashamed revelers represented dollar signs. As a newscaster, he had easy access to camera gear, and that prompted him to hatch a new business scheme.

When the ship was resting at anchor far from shore, Pat took photos of the carefree nudists, and the images soon appeared in adult magazines at corner newsstands throughout Southern California. These local publications were just the start. Pat had aspirations for going national. All he lacked were the right connections—underground sources who dared take on the unlawful task of distributing pornography across state lines.

"Can you put me in contact with someone you know?" Pat asked his close friend, George Chula.

"Why are you even pursuing this crazy business?" George countered. "Imagine if your wife and family ever found out!"

"I'm actually doing it for them, George!" Pat argued. "We've got living expenses and a mortgage that's overdue. It's only right that I support my family, don't you think?"

"That's your reasoning?" George asked, shaking his head. "You always were good at making up a story—to convince yourself at least, even if nobody else."

"You're darn right that's my reasoning, George! And I'm sure you'd do the same thing if you were me."

"I thought you knew me better," said George.

Pat didn't use his TV name in his adult publications. But his pride still led him to take a little credit for himself. He listed "Frances Patrick" as chief editor; Frances Patrick was Pat's birth name. Unless his mother happened to pick up a copy, his identity remained well protected.

Pat's pornographic business was risky. Transporting illegal products across state lines required shady deals with dangerous people.

Pat's secret life was growing darker by the day, but he still managed to maintain a wholesome image before the button-down community that trusted him. He faithfully attended mass every Sunday with his family. And to ensure his place in heaven, Pat wore his Saint Christopher medallion around his neck even while sleeping. He made his boys wear theirs, too. In Pat's mind, the Saint Christopher medal was more than a showy gold trinket. It indicated that his efforts to live a good life were endorsed by one of the church's most revered saints.

As a matter of Christian principle, Pat wouldn't even allow his daughters to date. "Not until you're eighteen!" he told them. And he meant it. Pat's public persona included ultraconservative values that he often articulated in editorials and public speeches.

The apparent incongruities in Pat's life fell at opposite ends of the moral spectrum. He resembled Billy Graham on one hand and Hugh Hefner on the other. Pat made no effort to hide his moral and righteous side, but the "Hefner" side remained sequestered behind closed doors, where secrets stayed buried and passions remained private. Only a select few saw Pat unrestrained.

Lois was not one of that select few.

The undercover Pat succumbed to forbidden desires, whereas the public Pat—the journalist—continued acting as the main moneymaker. Pat had built his reputation around his work, and he sought the respect every hardworking newsman deserves, nothing more, nothing less. Never did his dreams of journalistic notoriety include peddling illicit publications. For him, that low-life trade carried a deplorable stigma. Nevertheless, he now needed extra cash, not just to support his lavish public lifestyle, but also to support the increasing cost of clandestine philandering.

I'll give up the licentious stuff soon, he told himself.

His two personalities were entangled in so many ways that sometimes he nearly forgot which life he was living.

"The yacht's speedometer is on the blink," he said to Lois as he read the paper before work.

"How do you know?" Lois replied. "We haven't been out on the boat for weeks and weeks!"

"Oh... yeah," said Pat fumblingly. "I... um... I called Ralph at the club and asked him to take her out the other day, just to keep the gas from settling in the tank..."

He turned the page and rubbed his nose with a knuckle. "Hey! Look at this! A sale at Woolworth's!"

Lois looked at her husband and said nothing.

26

The Big Story

After his lengthy phone conversation with Morris Kominsky, station manager Joe Glotz was exuberant. With all its twists and turns, the Elsinore story was a guaranteed ratings winner. Joe was convinced that KTLA would receive endless praise for blowing the lid off the "evil government" that was terrorizing innocent Jews.

Joe replayed Kominsky's words in his head: Our public leaders cut off the healing water from the entire town. They left us dry and destitute. If that's not hatred and animus, what is? They deprived us of water! That's evil! That's torture!

What could be bigger news? The story brought to mind the greedy railroad moguls during the 1800s who forced landowners from their ranches and tortured the Chinese laborers who laid their tracks. Joe knew that KTLA would be foolish to reject this scoop.

And if anyone was daring enough for the Elsinore assignment, it was Pat Michaels. After challenging the Feds and defending mobster Mickey Cohen, Pat could take on anyone.

Pat listened as Joe explained. Then Pat spoke, "I need to talk to Kominsky right away. I want everything. Newspaper articles. Meeting minutes from city council. Notes from the property owners association, police reports, any correspondence to or from the health department. The whole ball of wax!"

Joe handed Pat a scrap of paper with Kominsky's number on it. Pat sat down and picked up the receiver, its rotary making a steady puttering noise as he dialed each digit. His chair squeaked as he leaned back and lit up a Kent.

While Pat listened to the phone ringing on the other end, Joe put his hands on the desk and leaned toward him. "This guy's a live one, Pat. He's wound tighter than a banjo string!"

"Let's just hope he didn't play you like a fiddle," Pat retorted. Joe's eyes narrowed as Pat's exhaled smoke surrounded them.

From the initial hello, it was obvious to Pat that Morris was jumpy. Even his breathing was abrupt, as if someone was holding a gun to his head while he spoke.

A few minutes into the conversation, Morris said, "Mr. Michaels, I appreciate your calling, but I believe it's best we meet in person. This phone line is likely tapped."

"I don't object to that," said Pat, even though he suspected Morris was delusional. "I prefer a face-to-face discussion anyway. Can you meet here at KTLA tomorrow?"

The next morning Morris showed up at the TV station. With him were Elsinore's newly elected mayor Thomas Bartlett and City Attorney Carl Kegley. Pat, Joe, and the three other men met in the conference room.

Bartlett and Kegley didn't talk much. They simply nodded supportively while Morris worked himself into an angry rant. It was plain to see that the battle had taken its toll on Kominsky. His face was red with anger as he recounted the plight of the property owners. When he finally finished his tale, he was breathing heavily and looked exhausted.

"Please forgive me," he said, dabbing his damp forehead with a handkerchief. "It's just that there's been so much violence and vandalism. It has me quite riled."

Pat raised his eyebrows. "Violence and vandalism?"

Morris looked at his hands. There was a long silence. At last Kegley explained in a dull monotone, "Somebody threw a rock through the stained-glass window at the synagogue."

"Broke the Ten Commandments!" Bartlett cried.

Pat clasped his Saint Christopher medal as if to protect the icon's holy ears from hearing the sacrilege.

"Even children are taking a beating," Bartlett continued.

"Jewish children!" Morris barked.

"This sounds like a dangerous assignment," Pat responded.

"No doubt about it. You should be deputized before your investigation begins," said Morris as he looked toward the mayor.

"We'll make sure Chief Bittle issues you a badge," Mayor Bartlett promised.

"Thanks," said Pat. "But a badge doesn't mean much without handcuffs and some fire power behind it."

"That can be arranged," the City Attorney told him, smiling for the first time that day.

27

Cold Cases

Having served on the front lines at Guadalcanal, Pat was fond of guns and he knew how to shoot. He happily took the pistol issued to him by Elsinore's Police Chief. It looked impressive, was preloaded, and badge and handcuffs were included. Pat felt even more important than usual. He had the one–two punch—his press card along with a police badge complete with heat. Now he could not only report from crime scenes, he could also act as arresting officer. If the suspect resisted, Pat was equipped for that, too.

"I just hope you'll never have to use this," Chief Bittle said gravely as he handed over the gun and shoulder holster.

"Time will tell. We'll see what happens," Pat responded.

Bittle eyed him suspiciously, and Pat hastily continued. "I agree with you, though. It would be better not to have to use force."

Pat had trouble concealing his excitement about his newfound authority in the town of Elsinore, and he struggled to maintain a somber face. "Thank you very much, Chief Bittle. I appreciate your confidence in me, and it won't be misplaced. I admire and respect this weapon you gave me, and believe me, I know how to use it safely."

"We prefer to us the term firearm, Mr. Michaels. We don't call it a weapon."

"Yes, yes. Of course. Whatever. By the way, Chief Bittle, now that this official deputizing business is complete, do you mind if I ask you a few questions?"

Bittle was by nature guarded when it came to the press, but he was also not immune to the spell of celebrity cast by the illustrious Pat Michaels. Small-town Elsinore had suddenly become big news, and Bittle fancied that some of the fame might rub off on him.

"Fire away," Bittle nodded. Then he suddenly realized that Pat was still holding the pistol. "I guess I should rephrase that!" he chuckled.

Pat looked at the gun and quickly tucked it away. "Thanks in advance for the interview, Chief!" he said. He signaled for the cameraman, who moved in closer. Pat reached into his black bag, grabbed his microphone, and flicked it on. After a quick sound check, he shouted, "Okay, Pete, roll the film!"

Facing the camera, Pat said, "I'm speaking to Elsinore's Police Chief Walter Bittle regarding recent events in this former resort town. Chief Bittle, could you recount for the TV audience the local hate crimes that have occurred, specifically those of an anti-Semitic nature?"

"Certainly," responded Chief Bittle. "One of the first instances occurred when two grown men accosted a young boy on his way home from school. They began by harassing him for being a Jew, and unfortunately the attack then turned physical. The child was beaten until senseless."

"Were the attackers arrested?" Pat asked.

"No," Bittle replied. "No suspects. No arrests. The case is still under investigation."

Pat reached for his Kent in the ashtray on the Chief's desk. By now the cigarette had smoldered to its filter, but Pat drew a lengthy drag of the foul nub anyway, smashed it back into the tray, and continued his interview.

"Tell me about the other incidents," Pat probed, aiming the microphone directly into Bittle's leathery face. Suddenly Bittle recoiled slightly as if noticing the mic for the first time. Self-awareness swept over him, and his lips trembled. Here he was, a law officer providing news footage for millions of TV viewers. It was serious business, and he realized his recorded words could be used against him later. Plus he feared looking foolish by proffering opinions and unsubstantiated rumors. He cleared his throat, hoping to calm his nerves and collect his thoughts.

Pat was all too familiar with the wide-eyed, frightened expression on Bittle's face. The best thing to do in these cases was to take a short break. He signaled the cameraman.

"Why don't you take a moment and get some water?" Pat suggested to Walter. "We'll roll whenever you're ready."

"I appreciate it," Bittle replied. "I'm sorry, sir. Thank you for your kindness. I just want to be sure I have these reports straight. This is my first TV interview."

"Cameras can be intimidating," Pat sympathized. "Anyway, I could use another smoke."

138

Bittle had regained his composure by the time the interview resumed. He recounted an abduction case that took place in July of 1956. According to reports, two Jewish women were kidnapped, taken to a remote location, and then beaten under a flaming cross. Pat listened with wide eyes.

"Were there any arrests following this incident?" Pat asked, hoping for an affirmative answer.

"No arrests," Bittle sighed. "No suspects. The case has gone cold."

"And I understand the synagogue was vandalized, too," Pat prodded.

"Obviously motivated by hate," Bittle affirmed. "A rock was thrown clear through the stained-glass window above the front entrance. Can't believe anyone would do such a thing. They literally broke the Ten Commandments. That was a dark day in Elsinore."

Anticipating the likely follow-up question, Bittle frowned, hating to repeat it: "No arrests. No suspects. Still under investigation."

Pat nodded dispassionately.

Bittle continued bitterly, "All we know is that Moses didn't break the commandments this time!"

"Well, we thank you for your answers Chief Bittle, and we wish you luck in your efforts to bring these culprits to justice."

Turning to the camera, Pat continued. "Ladies and gentlemen, this is your KTLA reporter Pat Michaels, speaking in Elsinore, California, with Police Chief Walter

Bittle. As the chief has related, Elsinore is a town rife with mysteries."

Pat paused for effect.

"And, sadly, Elsinore has become a city of hate."

28

Dust to Dust

When Pat's interview with Chief Bittle had ended, Kominsky and McGowan escorted Pat and his cameraman on a tour of Elsinore. As the four men walked from place to place, Morris and James provided a running commentary on the situation, naming every foe responsible for the devastation they saw. Without question, much of the once-beloved community was in disarray. Many areas resembled the ghost towns of the Wild West.

The wind kicked up a yellowish cloud of dust that hung over streets, buildings, and yards. Rain had come, but more was needed. The men could feel it in their nostrils. Elsinore was dry—dry and desolate.

"It's simple, Pat," Morris grumbled. "Jew haters wanted us out and they were willing to do anything to drive us away, even cut off our water."

Pat's heart sank at the thought. He had dropped out of high school to fight the Nazi threat. Hearing that the spirit of Hitler was alive and well in Elsinore made him sick to his stomach. The thick yellow air nauseated him even further. The deterioration in Elsinore reminded him of the smoking heaps he'd seen in cities after World War II.

Pat stuck a Kent between his lips, hoping that the smell of tobacco would help him forget the foul flashbacks of war.

"It pains me to say that those opposing us have succeeded in many ways," Morris remarked. "A lot of my people are already gone. Penniless, I might add. The enemies of the people can't get rid of me, though. We're going to fight this injustice. The town is supporting us now, plus we have every city seat in our hands. At this point, it's us against the state."

In Pat's mind, this part of the story didn't make sense. Of all places, why would the State Department of Health pick on Elsinore? Why was there such an interest in this tourist playground far out in the sticks? As the men continued their tour, the evidence in front of his eyes overcame Pat's doubts and questions. Morris's allegations were headline material, and that fact alone was enough to prompt a vigorous investigation.

Morris led the small group down Main Street. "Notice all the For Rent signs," he said. "It's been this way since the water was shut off. With the city now in shambles, no one wants to set up shop here anymore. It's killed our economy."

Pat looked at his cameraman to confirm that he was getting close-up shots; Pete was already on top of that.

There was no denying that the sights were shocking, and both Pat and Pete sensed the oppressive gloom over the city.

"I think I'm gonna need a cigarette after this," Pete mumbled.

Pat looked toward him. "Pete, you don't even smoke."

Before long, the four found themselves in front of Lake Theatre. The building was dilapidated and the surrounding lot was piled high with trash.

"In the past this movie house was the most popular place in town," James told them. "I used to bring my kids here. It's deserted now."

Pat looked up at the marquee. "It's obviously been deserted for some time," he observed. "I barely remember that movie."

Most of the letters were cracked and crooked, but all had survived. The merciless sun had also taken a toll on the marquee; it was oxidized to an eerie bone grey after years of neglect. Morris was quick to point out the irony. *The Screaming Skull*, he said sardonically. "Quite fitting, isn't it?"

Pat agreed, even though no one explained to him that the theatre didn't go out of business. On the contrary, it had moved to a new location just up the street. But rather than visit there, Morris led the group to more dire surroundings, where Elsinore's most popular tourist attraction now lay in ruins.

"The big draw here was the mineral pool," Morris related as they stood in front of the abandoned Elsinore Lake Lodge. "After that dried up, so did business. Owners were forced to shut down."

The men tramped through a tangle of weeds to an expansive patio area at the back of the lodge.

"There it is," Morris pointed. "That used to be the pool. It was the largest in Elsinore."

Pat looked at the sad scene. Nothing was left but a dusty, cracked basin filled with tumbleweeds.

"Do me a favor," James said, looking at Pat. "Don't smoke here. This place is a fire hazard."

The tour ended at the doorstep of the local synagogue. The damage was impossible to ignore, especially because the broken window was directly above the building's entrance. Pat didn't miss the irony here. The stained glass was installed at the front for good reason— so no one would overlook it. Vandals were never anticipated, but they hadn't overlooked it either. It had been years since the incident, but with Jews fleeing and membership declining, there was no money left to replace the glass. Cardboard and tape covered the hole in the beautiful window.

Pat's fingers lightly touched his forehead, belly, and shoulders. The sign of the cross.

Morris noticed Pat's religious gesture. Not wanting to be upstaged, he contemplated rending his garment—but his shirt was too expensive and he decided against it.

They left the synagogue and walked to Mava's Ice Cream Parlor, where each bought a five-cent Coke.

Late that night, Pat's typewriter clattered while other Sherman Oaks residents slept. The Elsinore exposé was birthing. Pat couldn't rest if he wanted to.

29
Fly by Night

"Congratulations, Mr. Michaels! You have successfully completed flight-school training! I'm pleased to present you with your pilot's license!" Pat accepted his certificate with glee.

Lois was witness to Pat's credentialing that evening. The kids were home with the babysitter. Pat was elated, nearly flying without a plane. Lois watched him shake hands with all his classmates, grabbing their arms and slapping them on their backs. When he finally looked over at her, she smiled wanly. "Congratulations," she mouthed silently.

Pat scowled briefly at Lois's lack of enthusiasm, but he didn't ponder her reaction for long. He turned back and continued kibitzing with his friends.

The timing was perfect for him to start flying. He had already made an offer on a private Cessna plane, and within days it was his. At last he could travel on a breeze from Los Angeles to Elsinore in a fraction of the time it took by car.

"This is a dream come true!" Pat told his wife. "We can really go places now!" As usual, Lois said little. She was afraid of the danger. She didn't trust Pat to keep them safe.

As it turned out, the children experienced severe vertigo when the plane was more than twenty feet off the ground. There were often tears and nausea in the air, and a couple of times Pat had to grab something he could use as an airsickness bag for his passengers.

This ain't no fun, Pat told himself. So much for family trips on this thing.

Pat didn't buy his plane primarily as a vehicle for family vacations anyway. Nor was he planning to use it chiefly for business. He mainly viewed it as yet another means of escape from banality so he could reengage his exciting secret life. "My Cessna," he breathed. Even the words exhilarated him.

"Well, our new toy has flopped for family recreation," he told Lois. "But you can't blame me. It's not my fault it makes the kids upchuck."

The plane did score high when it came to commuting though. No longer would he waste precious time in earthbound traffic. The small news crew could land at their destination in a matter of minutes. This allowed Pat extra time to work on the Elsinore story.

With the hours Pat saved each day, he easily met all his deadlines. Not only was there enough film footage for a segment on The Big Three broadcast, but Pat also began to envision a full-hour documentary. Plus Morris promised Pat all the financial backing he needed, compliments of the Elsinore Property Owners Association. "That's an offer I can't refuse!" Pat told Kominsky.

To save even more time as he worked on the story, Pat hand-carried reels of film to the production studio. The project was progressing swimmingly.

146

"City of Hate!" he announced with satisfaction as a giant puff of smoke escaped his lungs.

"Excuse me?" replied a confused editor.

"City of Hate!" Pat declared triumphantly. "I want it in large, bold letters. The film is called *City of Hate.*"

Most of the film footage had landed in a heap on the cutting-room floor, but the end product was pithy and substantive. This was the making of an award-winning documentary. With testimonies of abuse, abductions, and anti-Semitism, *City of Hate* would easily secure KTLA's place as frontrunner in evening news.

Although the potential payoff was huge, there were risks. After all, Pat was making allegations against government agencies for persecuting innocent Jews and cutting off people's water supply. These were serious charges.

After the initial preview, however, station manager Joe Glotz gave him a ringing endorsement. "You can't make this stuff up!" he exclaimed.

Far be it from me to argue with the boss! thought Pat. He just nodded and smiled.

30

Sheer Hysteria

Morris Kominsky suggested promoting *City of Hate* within the Jewish community in advance of the broadcast. "A small city like Elsinore can't fight the State of California alone. It'd be like attacking a rhino with a flyswatter. Listen Pat, you have to start drumming up support by contacting the Anti-Defamation League. They've already looked into the situation."

Indeed they had, but ADL representatives weren't prepared to sign-off on anything blindly, not even when the KTLA publicity manager called them.

"Your support would mean a great deal to us," Claudia Bowman urged over the phone.

"That's not going to happen," ADL Regional Director Milton Senn remarked.

"I did mention I'm calling on behalf of Channel 5, didn't I?"

"Your point is?" Senn said dryly.

"We have a reputable news department, not to mention the largest viewing audience in Southern California," Claudia continued.

Media credentials did not impress Milton. "Exactly!" he burst out. "And for that reason alone it's best that we maintain a safe distance. Unless we can actually preview the film, we are denying your request. We can't support it. We can't endorse it. We can't risk having our name smeared on something we know nothing about—not with thousands of people watching!"

"The entire KTLA news staff stands behind *City of Hate*," Claudia ventured. "It sheds light on how the Jewish community is often mistreated, even terrorized in some instances. We hope to bring not only awareness, but swift change. I'd think that you would…"

"I'll tell you what needs to change!" Milton shot back. "The title of your broadcast. *City of Hate*? Are you kidding me? I can't think of anything more despicable! We have also looked into this situation. Yes, there are problems in Elsinore like any other city, but by no means is it a city of hate. If this is the message you hope to convey, don't expect support from the ADL. We clearly do not share the views and opinions of KTLA regarding the Elsinore conflict. Put that in your documentary."

Claudia fumbled for words. Well, Mr. Senn, of course. We're sorry you feel that way, but…"

"Yes, I do feel that way, Miss… Miss…"

"Bowman."

"Yes, Miss Bowman. That's how I feel. And, as you know, I speak for our entire organization. So I thank you for calling. And I urge you to reconsider your plans to go forward with this project."

"Well, I… We…"

"Good day, Miss Bowman." Senn hung up and Claudia was left with a dead receiver in her hand.

Some special-interest groups were eventually invited to a *City of Hate* preview, but local ADL representatives were not included. Pat made sure of that. Claudia's description of Milton's remarks had angered and offended him. *City of Hate* was Pat's baby. He had worked hard to make the documentary as perfect as possible, and he couldn't jeopardize its success by some ADL muckety-muck who might cause a scene at the preview.

Furthermore, Pat felt strongly about the show's title. "I refuse to be challenged about that name," he told his colleagues. "I don't care if some people think it's overly sensational. The name *City of Hate* makes a statement. It's the truth, doggone it, and people need to know!"

Pat's unselfish regard for the downtrodden masked his real motive for sticking with the title: it would guarantee high ratings.

The preview caused a large buzz in the Jewish community, and Milton quickly learned of it. He immediately called the KTLA general manager. "I demand a private showing!" he cried.

"Well, sir," the manager said, "our production deadlines are tight, and we're all booked up for the rest of this week and into the next it seems. We'd need a team to arrange another showing, and we have no extra personnel at the moment. We're stretched very thin here."

"That's fine," said Senn. "My lawyer will call you within twenty-four hours." The conversation ended.

KTLA arranged a preview just for Senn, who insisted on bringing Joseph Roos of the Jewish Federation–Council's Community Relations Committee. Both sat stone-faced as they watched the program. After the closing credits, Milton stood up and turned to the projectionist and news staff. "The entire content must be overhauled. It's reprehensible. And lose that title!" he shouted as he stormed out of the room.

When interviewed by the Anglo-Jewish weekly paper Heritage, Milton stated, "Charges that the Jews of Elsinore are terrorized, live in fear and trepidation, and that the city itself seethes with anti-Jewish hostility, which 'parallels the nightmare of Nazi Germany with frightening fidelity,' is sheer hysteria."

Milton went on to say, "Mr. Michaels asserted that the Jews of Elsinore—who number about 400 out of a total population of 2300—were given six months to get out of Elsinore or there would be bloodshed. This is fiction. At another point Mr. Michaels said that the Jews of Elsinore were given six months to get out of the city or be killed. This, too, is fiction."

Regardless of how members of the ADL felt, or how adamantly opposed Milton was to the content, no alterations were made to Pat's hour-long documentary. Nor was the title changed. *City of Hate* was broadcast twice "as is" in December 1959.

Pat and Lois watched the second showing in their living room. Afterward Pat chirped, "How do you like that, Lois! Another big success for the best newscaster in Southern California! Chalk up a riveting exposé to my growing list of accomplishments! I can't wait to see what's in store for me after this. I swear, I have a charmed life, don't you think so? I'm a legend already!"

"Pat..." began Lois. "I think..."

"I have to go to the backyard office for the rest of the evening to finish up some things. I have that big trip coming up, you know. Thanks for watching my masterpiece! Say good-night to the kids."

Pat walked out the back door, and Lois sat crying in her wingback chair.

31

In Other Headlines

"Jewish Population in California Resort City Reported Terrorized," screamed the front page of the *Jewish Telegraphic Agency* on Christmas Eve 1959. The article read:

> "The KTLA television station here has aired an hour-long documentary program asserting that a nearby resort city, Elsinore, was on a verge of violence against its Jewish citizens. Officials of the station said that to get the report, Pat Michaels and other members of the station's news staff were sworn in as members of Elsinore's police force 'for their own safety.'
>
> "A KTLA special news release, announcing the *City of Hate* program, declared that the news staff had 'uncovered a situation which parallels the nightmare of Nazi Germany with frightening fidelity.' It stressed that 'the terrorism is part of a calculated campaign designed to drive out the large Jewish population which has gathered in the resort city.' The documentary was shown twice.

"The program showed that damage had been done to synagogues and centers in Elsinore, which is 72 miles southeast of Los Angeles. The news staff interviewed officials and residents of Elsinore to determine their reactions to widening signs of anti-Semitism. These included threatening letters, wall inscriptions and stonings. The program charged that a concealed organization, calling itself the International Freedom Fighters, was responsible.

"Originally Elsinore's tourist trade was based on a large lake. When the lake dried up, there was a large influx of elderly Jews who were attracted by the area's mineral waters. The mineral waters were cut off on contention that it had high fluoride content, but Elsinore residents expressed the belief in statements on the KTLA program that this was a device to drive Jewish businessmen out of the area.

"Mr. Michaels contended on the program that a measure approved at the last session of the California Legislature to refill Lake Elsinore was a direct cause of the current campaign of intimidation. He said that the goal was to scare Jewish residents out and regain property sold to them during the area's depressed period."

The *Jewish Telegraphic Agency* wasn't the only media outlet to report the controversy surrounding *City of Hate*. News of the hour-long broadcast was widespread. Pat's colleague Clete Roberts was especially curious about the International Freedom Fighters, and he investigated the group further.

154

"You'll never believe this," Clete told Pat a few days later. "The *International Freedom Fighters* are anticommunists with headquarters in Elsinore. The group is extremely vocal against the Elsinore Progressive League. And, of course, the EPL has been blacklisted by the FBI's big cheese—J. Edgar Hoover himself!"

Pat looked at Clete incredulously. "Clete, you know that I've been living this stuff for months. I'm well aware of the IFF and Hoover's opinion of the EPL. Where do you think I've been?"

"I just wondered if you knew, Pat," Clete retorted. "That's all I'm saying."

Pat swiveled away toward his typewriter while Clete stared for several seconds at the back of Pat's head. Finally Clete returned to his own work as well.

Clete had also discovered that, although the Feds eventually backed off their investigation of EPL's communistic ties, they continued to surveil two of its members—Morris Kominsky and James McGowan. And the Feds were also wary of Michaels' ties to the two men. The FBI was convinced that Morris and James were using Pat to publically accuse the Freedom Fighters—and the California Department of Health—of being co-conspirators in the effort to oust Elsinore's Jews.

Was this true? Was Pat a pawn in a larger plot perpetrated by the communists in Elsinore? Or was Pat himself a major player helping to propel events in Elsinore for his own gain? Clete wanted to trust Pat's integrity, but he had his doubts.

City of Hate also fueled further attention from SUAC. In addition to the committee's efforts to find the truth, Attorney General Stanley Mosk called for a separate investigation. As the first Jewish American appointed to the position of AG, Mosk had a personal interest in the Elsinore case. Ultimately, it was Mosk's involvement that paved way for the grand jury investigation.

The first weekend of January 1960, Pat took the *Bon Michelle* on another solo voyage into the Pacific. His aim was to meet his secretary at their usual secret hideaway, but before he reached his destination, a fierce storm hit the ship. The winds howled, the waves crashed over the bow, and blinding rain pelted the craft. For the first time as captain of his ship, Pat became seasick as he tried to steer the heaving craft back to the Balboa Bay Club. When he finally made it to shore two hours later, he stumbled to the dock, found his Buick in the lot, and drove home.

The storm at sea that evening was nothing compared to the storm that was about to hit his life.

32
Hopelessly Entangled

With his reputation in jeopardy and state investigators closing in on him, Pat was unnerved. He called Attorney George Chula. After all, Pat thought, George told me he owed me one, and now it's time to collect.

Certainly George would remember Pat's unrelenting efforts to help save murderer Billy Rupp. How could George have made history without Pat's help? George had wanted Pat to contact the original jury that had sentenced Billy to die. Pat had managed to locate each jury member for George.

"Now it's my head on the chopping block," Pat mumbled as he dialed. "How quickly things change."

"Hello?" answered George.

"Hello George. How are you doing?"

"Fine, Pat. You?"

"George, listen. I'm in a bind. I'm ready to collect on your promise," Pat told him.

"Excuse me?"

"Remember the jurors in the Rupp case?" Pat said.

"I thought we settled that score when I gave you a lead on Lynn Stuart."

"George, come on. That wasn't much of a lead. I told you that before," Pat reminded him. "To be honest, you barely gave me the time of day. But during the Rupp case, I invested countless hours helping you."

"I know, Pat," George admitted. "I just like giving you a hard time. What do you need? I imagine it has to do with your documentary. Word has it, you've made the DA's hit list!"

Pat swallowed hard. News was spreading fast. "George, you've hit the nail on the head. District Attorney Mosk blatantly rejected everything we described in *City of Hate*. It's not helping me that California's most prominent Jewish official is directly challenging my findings and reporting."

George shook his head silently. He knew enough about Mosk to understand that he was a respected public servant with a reputation for putting facts above feelings. Mosk didn't hide his Jewish heritage, and he was proud to support his people. He would normally defend the Jews without hesitation. Despite that loyalty, Stanley Mosk was not one who was swayed by hype or hysteria. Nor would he tolerate TV reporters who dared exploit the Jews for the sake of their big stories.

As Mosk stated in his report, anti-fluoride and anti-Semitism became "hopelessly entangled." Mosk was of the opinion that the KTLA documentary was fabricated. He further stated: "It is natural that people in a community with Elsinore's problems can become somewhat emotional in interpreting unusual events. It is disturbing when outside commentators encourage distortion and exaggeration."[1]

After Pat explained his dilemma to his friend, George said, "I'll see what I can do."

The two men hung up. If anyone can help me, it's George, Pat told himself.

But the noose was tightening. Not only was the legal system bearing down on Pat, but his job was on shaky ground too. Clete lost confidence in Pat and insisted that Joe Glotz terminate him immediately. Paramount Pictures, owners of the station, also demanded answers. Suddenly Pat's colleagues were deserting him and his formerly bright future looked bleak.

Would KTLA stand by him? Would he be blacklisted in the Southern California market? These questions led Pat quickly to update his resume. He had a lot riding on his large income. In addition to his excessive lifestyle, his mistress and his freelance pornography business were draining his finances.

Unaware of his misbehavior, Lois remained faithful to Pat, standing by his side in the midst of the storms. At times it felt unmanageable. Pat controlled his emotions at work, but he unloaded his frustrations when he arrived home. His temper often blew out of control, sometimes to the point of violence. A couple of fist holes in the walls showed evidence of the domestic disturbances. Through it

---

[1] Jacqueline R. Braitman and Gerald F. Uelmen: *Justice Stanley Mosk: A Life at the Center of California Politics and Justice*, McFarland, 2012, page 98.

all, Lois maintained her love for Pat. She hated his tantrums, but she dutifully kept forgiving him.

Pat realized the treasure he had in Lois, but he still found time to nuzzle in the arms of his secretary. Even his secret sweetheart, though, could not deliver Pat from the scandal he had created for himself. George Chula was his last hope.

"I haven't forgotten," George assured the troubled journalist the next time he spoke to Pat. "I'm working on it. I told you I owed you one, and I said I'd do all I could do. Like you, Pat, I am a man of my word. Don't you ever forget it!"

With so much attention on the Elsinore case, the payload for George would come later. Even if Pat were dragged through the mud during his ordeal, George would come out on top. George would make sure of that. With all the media coverage, Chula's name would be in lights. And for George, his own success was all that really mattered.

33

Scandal

After *City of Hate* aired, the target on Pat's back grew larger by the day. He had leveled serious charges against high-profile government agencies. It was one thing for Pat to accuse the Department of Health of conspiring to drive Jews out of Elsinore by denying the town of its water. It was another matter for Pat to accuse the State Attorney General's Office of aiding in the conspiracy.

Pat alleged that the Attorney General used illegal devices to spy on prominent members of Elsinore's Property Owners Association. Exposing the POA's suspected communist ties was an underhanded attempt to "whitewash the anti-Semitic aspect of the problem," according to Pat.

The accusations didn't end there. Pat claimed that state agencies deliberately exaggerated the dangers of fluoride. "Most cities are fighting to add fluoride to their water," he asserted in the broadcast. No specifics were provided, but the documentary assured its audience that fluoride dangers were fabricated for purposes of evil.

"The problem in Elsinore is one of greed," Pat declared, "brought about by a small minority that are the masterminds behind the organized project to rid by terror the Jews from the city." He went on to say, "We know who they are, or at least who some of them are, and we are willing to turn our files over to the proper law-enforcement agencies who will protect the constitutional rights of the people of that city."

Pat's claims of scandal prompted the state to initiate a full-scale investigation. Neither the Attorney General nor the State Senate was about to let Pat make such charges without a fight. While SUAC pursued its investigation, the Attorney General's office conducted its own. Each agency was determined to expose the communist aspect of the problem and prove that Pat was a conspirator.

After several visits to Elsinore, each involving multiple interviews, the Attorney General's office issued a written report dated April 4, 1960. The findings in this report drastically differed from the charges made in *City of Hate*. These findings were included in a much lengthier dossier issued by SUAC.

The Attorney General's report traced the history of the water controversy and pointed out that there were two radical groups: those alleged to be Communists by legislative committees, and those who were anti-Semitic agitators. Each group had gathered a small following and had engaged in protracted campaigns of vituperation. A larger group confused anti-Semitism with anti-Communism, and a group of militant Jews reacted by accusing both groups of being anti-Semitic.

Regarding KTLA's *City of Hate* program, the Attorney General reported:

Examples of the program's allegations and the facts are set forth below:

"Almost every other building in Elsinore has a for rent sign." There were five store buildings for rent at this time. In 1955–1956, Elsinore's most prosperous year, there were eleven stores vacant.

"These are the sunbaked streets that give you a feeling of emptiness…" Doubtless, some of this feeling of emptiness was caused by the televising of Spring Street on a Sunday morning when the business district was practically deserted. Both sides of the street are marked with No Parking At Any Time signs.

"There's the empty, desolate theatre in the heart of the city, whose lobby once held people; now only trash and waste collect." The empty, desolate theatre was abandoned after condemnation some years ago, and a new theatre was built around the corner by the same owner.

"And there are signs of vanished wealth, a wealth that once was that of Elsinore when it was a tourist playground and a world-famous mineral spa. But the city's swimming pools are empty except for collections of rotting tumbleweeds. The water is gone." In the pool pictured on the program, the water is gone. The pool was abandoned some thirty-five years ago after the dressing rooms burned.

"Now there's plenty of evidence that doom, the doom of a town that is decaying, dying, being choked to death, is running rampant." Although the motels have been hurt by the tourist exodus, fourteen new homes are under construction at this time. Building permits for 1958 had an aggregate value of $182,642. The total for 1959 was $445,797.

Sales tax receipts show an increase from $26,653 in 1957 to $27,755 in 1959.

More serious were the program's charges about acts of violence aimed at Elsinore's Jewish residents. Examples from the AG's report include:

"And a Jew told me how his child was beaten on his way home from school by adults who cursed him as a Jew." No one in Elsinore knows of the beating of any child. Investigation revealed that the father of one child told of an incident involving his son to the program coordinator. He is certain that his story was the basis of the allegation about the beating of the boy. The boy says he has never been cursed or insulted for being a Jew by anyone in Elsinore.

"There in the yellowing newspaper files you can find some of the background. You can find the story of the two Jewish women who were kidnapped on the streets years ago, taken to a vacant lot, and beaten under a flaming cross." In July 1956, two women were the victims of an unsuccessful purse-snatching effort. One was struck several times by one of the two assailants. The newspaper clipping refers also to another assault in a neighboring town a week earlier where $30 and a watch were taken by two young men after striking their victim in a similar manner. The description given by the Elsinore woman at that time to the attending physician tallied with that of the assailants in the earlier case. There was no kidnapping and no fiery cross.

"But its biggest pride was shattered by an anti-Semitic vandal this past week. The costly stained glass window, which was the congregation's pride and joy, was shattered by a rock… But if anything hurt them the most, these people, it was the rock through their prized stained glass window, the rock that shattered the Ten Commandments."

The "anti-Semitic vandal" was a 16-year-old boy, who, in the company of two other 16-year-olds, was returning from a football game about six weeks before the TV broadcast on November 6, 1959. While en route to the bus station they were chasing each other through the park, which is directly across the street from the synagogue. One of the boys tackled the other who fell on a rock. The latter picked up the rock, which had hurt him, and aimlessly threw it. When they heard glass break, the boys ran off. The boy who threw the rock comes from a poor family. He wanted to report the incident the next day but became frightened when he read in the newspaper that window was valued at $125. His story has been corroborated by other persons and our independent investigation. He had no realization that he had hit a synagogue window across the park until the next day.

SUAC concurred with the Attorney General's findings, indicating in their report[2]:

> ...on examining the TV allegations and the actual facts, instance after instance, one might be tempted to dismiss Elsinore's anti-Semitism as pure fiction. There is, however, a serious amount of anti-Semitism in Elsinore. It merits further investigation, despite the *City of Hate* presentation.
>
> At this point grave allegations have been made concerning the motives and methods of the opposed groups. It is charged that there is an organized conspiracy to drive the Jews from Elsinore. It is likewise alleged that this charge itself is part of a Communist scheme to create strife by raising the issue of religious hatred and racial intolerance.
>
> It is impossible to determine the actual truth regarding these allegations of conspiracy without putting those making these statements under oath. Charge and countercharge will succeed each other until there is an opportunity to get at the truth.

With such obvious discrepancies surrounding the Elsinore saga, state officials were more determined than ever to prosecute all parties responsible for the numerous tall tales of anti-Semitism and government conspiracy.

---

[2] California Senate Fact-finding Committee on Un-American Activities, Eleventh Report, pages 179, 180.

The big targets were those liable for misleading the general public. And Pat Michaels topped that list.

"This documentary is backfiring and boomeranging on me in a really bad way," Pat told Rhonda his secretary after work one day. "I'm afraid of what's going to happen to me."

He was hoping Rhonda would assure him, encourage him, and tell him everything would be all right.

"Yeah," she said. "I'm afraid too."

34

Shaky Ground

Pat had said so himself. He had announced it loudly on *City of Hate*, and then he'd repeated the claim in a separate broadcast on April 7, 1960: "We know who they are, or at least who some of them are, and we are willing to turn our files over to the proper law-enforcement agencies who will protect the constitutional rights of the people of that city." Apparently, the state-appointed Grand Jury wasn't viewed as a "proper law-enforcement agency"—not by Pat or his legal counsel anyway. When the Grand Jury demanded evidence, Pat refused to comply. Attorney George Chula further advised him against answering any questions.

Thus the Grand Jury found Pat to be an "evasive and irresponsible witness," reporting that "Mr. Michaels did not identify anybody who was a so-called 'mastermind' nor did he produce any evidence to support his allegations in that regard. Further, Michaels, while offering on the telecast to turn over his files... actually delayed the Grand Jury investigation into the whole matter for a period of five months through his legal maneuvering. If Michaels had, in fact, any genuine information about any possible violence to be inflicted on any citizens of the City of Elsinore, it would have been his duty to present such information to the Grand Jury at once in the interest of justice."[3]

---

[3] Michaels v. Superior Court, 184 Cal. App. 2d 820 - Cal: Court of Appeal 1960.

Pat's unwillingness to cooperate led to swift action from his accusers. In a summons to appear before the Riverside County Supreme Court, Michaels was ordered to "…show cause, if any he has, as to why he should not be deemed in contempt of Court for refusal to answer questions propounded to him by the Riverside County Grand Jury … and be punished according to law."

George Chula cited the First, Fourth, Fifth, and Fourteenth Amendments to the United States Constitution. He failed to persuade the court. Judge John Gabbert upheld the Grand Jury decision for punishment. Chula petitioned the motion, accusing Gabbert of prejudice. To his dismay, the petition went unheard. He had filed too late.

By January 1961, the Grand Jury had voted indictments against not only Pat Michaels, but also against Elsinore City Council members who were now skattering from their elected positions like roaches on a hot skillet. Included in the indictments were City Attorney Carl Kegley, Mayor Thomas Bartlett, Police Chief Walter Bittle, POA President Morris Kominsky, and Kominsky's fellow instigators James McGowan and Sam Farber.

Council members were indicted with "conspiracy to violate the terms of the city's water permit from the State Department of Public Health," whereas Attorney Kegley was charged with "attempting to defraud the City of Elsinore by presenting false claims."

Attached to these actions was a twenty-page document in which the Grand Jury condemned the "highly inflammatory and irresponsible nature of the [*City of Hate*] telecast." It was further stated "…the chief of police of the city of Elsinore has ties with private citizens in that town which are totally out of harmony with sound objective policing methods." This remark served to draw attention to communist instigators, most notably Morris Kominsky and James McGowan.

In a reaction against contaminating influences, the Grand Jury proposed that the City of Elsinore contract out law enforcement to the Riverside County Sheriff's Office for "adequate policing of the community." Outsourcing would also prevent any spontaneous or haphazard issuing of badges to members of the media or to others with "inflammatory and irresponsible" tendencies.

Shortly after the Grand Jury indictments were issued, SUAC submitted the results of their investigation of subversive activity in Elsinore. Their report stated:

> From the time that its attention was directed to the trouble at Elsinore in 1958 until the return of the indictments by the Riverside County Grand Jury in 1961, this Committee has sent investigators into the area on five separate occasions, each of the visits lasting for several days. Naturally, our interest was to ascertain the extent and influence of subversive infiltration in the community. In passing, however, we revert to the findings of the Grand Jury and the State Attorney General's Office relating to anti-Semitism, and corroborate each report completely by our own independent findings that, while there certainly was an anti-Semitic feeling in the community, it was manifested by a very small group of people, magnified out of all true proportions, and

certainly amounted to no plot for the purpose of ridding the city of its Jewish residents. It must be borne in mind, also, that it is the business of the Anti-Defamation League of the B'nai B'rith to deal with anti-Semitism and that the B'nai B'rith declared the KTLA telecast of the situation presented an entirely erroneous and highly magnified concept of anti-Semitism at Elsinore.[4]

The questions surrounding the Elsinore story continued to gain widespread attention in Southern California, leaving few convinced of the claims made in *City of Hate*. With diminishing support from the Jewish community, KTLA had no choice but to reexamine the veracity of their controversial broadcast.

Anchorman Clete Roberts confronted Pat in the KTLA's parking lot late one afternoon.

"Michaels," he called to Pat. "You know, don't you, that I've talked to Glotz. I told him that I'm distancing myself completely from you. I hate to say it, but I can't team up with someone who broadcasts fraudulent stories and ginned-up hype. If viewers no longer see us as honest, well… then… we have nothing."

"Clete, listen…" Pat stammered, stepping toward him with outstretched palms.

"Joe completely agrees with me, Pat," Clete continued. "How could you do it? You're not only ruining your own reputation, but you're bringing down this whole

---

[4] California Senate Fact-finding Committee on UnAmerican Activities, Eleventh Report, pages 182–183.

station with your lies and propaganda. Heads are going to roll, Pat. Heads will roll. I've worked too hard for someone to throw it away for me. I have a career to consider… and a family."

Hot guilt and shame washed over Pat. His mouth was dry and his stomach churned. He stood in the setting California sun, paralyzed, as another friend turned and walked away.

35
The Real Trouble

No one was surprised when the Grand Jury recommended a revamp of law enforcement in Elsinore. Cries of police corruption came even from the officers. The SUAC report noted: "Former members of the Elsinore Police Department have stated that the residents of that city 'had the wool pulled over their eyes by Communist agitators who had been moving into the city for the last three years.'"

SUAC investigators agreed with these officers, stating:

> ...at least thirty-five of the most active agitators and propagandists, who participated in the effort to get control of the city government of Elsinore, have long and persistent records of Communist front affiliation and similar agitation in other localities. Many of the voters in the municipal election that resulted in the ouster of the old officials and their replacement with new ones backed by the Property Owners Association had moved into Elsinore—despite rumors of political and economic disaster in that city—from Los Angeles just in time to be eligible to vote in the election.

SUAC investigators did not deny that anti-Semitism was evident in Elsinore. However, communist agitators had caused even more trouble. The SUAC report noted:

The reports of anti-Semitism were highly exaggerated, as is seen from the report of the Riverside County Grand Jury and the investigative report submitted by the State Attorney General's office. Nevertheless, there was anti-Semitism to some degree, and this regrettable state of affairs, together with the economic and political controversies, provided an ideal situation for the Communist leaders to move in and exploit to the utmost. Kominsky and McGowan were in constant contact with their superiors from Los Angeles, and checks of automobile license numbers disclosed the character of persons with whom they were doing business.

Morris Kominsky and James McGowan were recognized experts in the American political tradition of creating mountains from molehills. But the mountain they made in Elsinore became a volcano. When it finally erupted, an entire city was scorched.

According to SUAC:

The situation in Elsinore is, in our view, far from settled. As long as highly indoctrinated Communist agitators reside in the area the trouble will continue, and we are hopeful that the exposure of the leaders of the pro-Communist element in that little city will put a stop to their ability to take advantage of a local controversy for the purpose of agitating, recruiting and propagandizing for their own ulterior motives.

SUAC officials anticipated challenges from the communists, and the organization documented these expectations:

> From the group of residents with Communist front affiliations, and their supporters, we can anticipate charges of red-baiting, witch-hunting, McCarthyism, destruction of civil liberties, irresponsible charges, and all of the shopworn and threadbare propaganda devices that are always emitted by persons whose subversive records are finally dragged out into the daylight. In the meantime the appeal from the Superior Court decision quashing the Grand Jury indictments is pending, and the situation in Elsinore is being closely observed by several official agencies.

The media turned against Pat Michaels, and SUAC's opinion was widely accepted as fact. Only jittery alarmists were still haunted by the allegations made in *City of Hate*. As for the citizens of Elsinore, most felt duped by their newly elected representatives. Reporters read embarrassing doom-and-gloom diatribes on TV, and residents became increasingly ashamed of the horrible reputation surrounding their city. The scandalous KTLA documentary had hurt and humiliated Elsinore. A series of torturous aftershocks followed the broadcasts, and every rude jolt set the struggling city back further from the rebound it desperately needed.

The year was 1960. A gallon of gas cost 25 cents. Former mayor Cheryl French filled up her tank and drove away from Elsinore forever.

36

Holy Places

One thing remained constant in Pat's turbulent life: he diligently took his family to Mass every Sunday. The girls didn't mind, but the boys rebelled, whined, argued, and cried while Lois scrubbed their faces and combed their hair. She alternately admonished and cajoled them as they dressed in their starchy white shirts, plaid jackets, and neck-choking ties.

"Where the heck are they?" Pat asked, looking at his watch as he waited in the driver's seat of his recently purchased Chevy Corvair Monza. He honked the horn.

After several minutes and many complaints, the car doors finally slammed and they backed out of the driveway, heading down the winding road from Sherman Oaks Hills to *Saint Cyril's Catholic Church* in Encino. The small car was hot and confining, and the irritated boys pushed and kicked with polished shoes against the backs of the front seats. Lois held her tongue as the seat bounced behind her. Pat was less patient.

"Quit kicking my seat or I'll jump back there and tan your ever-loving hides!" he barked. The boys stopped kicking, recognizing that they had pushed Dad far enough. But their pouts and scowls didn't leave their faces all morning.

The car was uncomfortable, but the ancient pews at in the dank and stuffy cathedral were even worse. Pat and his family slid into the back row so no one would notice their lateness. The boys squirmed, whimpered, and whispered through the entire service. The Michaels family was always the last to arrive and the first to leave.

The family was slinking out the door after service one Sunday when Pat felt a tap on his shoulder. He turned to see Father Lawlor.

"Good morning, Mr. Michaels," said the Holy Reverend.

"Well, Father Lawlor! How are you? Wonderful service. Thank you so much for all…"

"Mr. Michaels, I was hoping to talk with you briefly," the priest intoned.

"Lois, take the kids to the car and wait for me," Pat told his wife tersely.

Pat faced the Father and smiled nervously. "What can I do for you Monsignor?"

"Mr. Michaels, you have been very influential in the community. As you know, people are watching you and your family carefully. And when you come to Mass late and leave early, it doesn't make a good impression on our parishioners." Pat's mouth fell open, but nothing came out.

"Plus, I haven't seen you at confession recently, and I think you may have missed Holy Communion, too."

"Well, Father, my job takes me away sometimes, on the weekends… you know. My hours are unpredictable."

"Pat, jobs come and jobs go. But missing Mass is a mortal sin. Your eternal destiny is at stake. Be careful Mr. Michaels!" he said ominously.

"I'm so sorry, Father Lawlor. I didn't realize how you felt..."

"It's not just how I feel, it's what the Church states! You know, KNXT anchor Jerry Dunphy has a similarly busy job, and he's always here, sitting in the front pew to hear the liturgy. Jerry is prompt to church, even when his job takes him to the desert or to the sea."

Pat swallowed in discomfort as Lawlor eyed him coldly.

"Father, Father!" cried a woman behind the Reverend. "I must speak to you about the flowers! Our usual florist will be closed next week! What shall we do?"

During the diversion, Pat walked quickly down the stone steps, got in the car, and peeled out of the parking lot.

As the weeks passed, Pat spent less and less time at home. His calendar was continuously clogged by reporting the news, conferring with lawyers, and dodging authorities.

"Our children need a father," Lois told him at breakfast one morning.

"Lois, how could you even doubt that I'm here for the kids? They're the reason for all my sacrifices!" He folded up the newspaper and pushed back his chair. "So please tell them for me that I'm here for them!" he said as he left the house.

Pat would not take a break from his busyness. Nor would he pull away from the *Bon Michelle* and his secret shipmate. Both became ready escapes from his mounting woes. He told his mistress he'd never leave her. He promised Lois the same thing. He'd swear on a Bible that both statements were true—but swearing they were true didn't make them so.

The next time Lois questioned him, Pat wept real tears. "How could you think I'd fall for someone else?"

"You're constantly gone," Lois averred.

"I'm busy with work!"

"At 2:00 in the morning with Rhonda?"

"What are you implying?" Pat argued.

"You're spending time with her when you should be with me!"

"Shame on you for your insinuation! I told you, we're working!" Pat was fuming. The tears in his eyes turned to fire, and cigarette smoke shot from his nostrils like a dragon.

"All I'm saying is, you spend more time with your secretary than with me. I'm your wife after all, not her."

"Lois, you're paranoid. You need to trust me. You're my one and only. After all these years don't you know that? Geez!"

Despite his undercover escapades, Pat behaved as a decent father when at home. He often amused the kids with a curious pet ghost. Its puppet strings vanished into the darkness once the lights went out. All that was visible was a glowing ball beneath a floating white handkerchief. The neighborly spook would fly from child to child, wooing

180

each with affection, reminding the kids of the popular *Casper the Friendly Ghost* cartoon.

Movie nights in the basement were equally fun. Pat would gather the family in front of the TV for scary showings of *Frankenstein*, *Dracula*, or *The Werewolf*. Bowls of popcorn and Reese's Peanut Butter Cups were passed around; the candy had been donated to KTLA in appreciation for The Big Three's advertising.

When the kids were sick, it was like Christmas. Pat was sympathetic to every ailment, and he always brought gifts to whoever was lucky enough to run a fever. As might be expected, the boys frequently exaggerated their sufferings, and Dad would reward them with a new Tonka Toy Truck or a Red Ryder rifle. Pat never questioned whether faking was involved. He loved spoiling his kids, in part to compensate for his frequent absences. The little ones never complained, but the gifts failed to soothe Lois's concerns.

Whether it was on his children or on himself, Pat loved to spend. Mostly on himself, and usually more than he could afford. He loved expensive toys, boats, planes, campers, and fancy cars. With creditors now after him, these luxuries began to slip away one by one.

"Daddy, where'd your car go?" young Terrance asked him after the Thunderbird was repossessed.

"The devil took it!" Pat declared as if he really believed it.

The devil not only wanted Pat's car. Eventually he snatched away the KTLA job as well.

"I'm sorry, Pat," Joe Glotz told him. "I'm only following directives from above. It's out of my hands."

"Yeah. Thanks a lot, Joe," Pat muttered. "I know Clete has a hand in this. Plus, I know where your directives are from. Not from above. They're from below!" He gave Joe a thumb's down gesture.

Pat was heartbroken and angry. Everything was crumbling, and it wasn't his fault. Father Lawlor's right, he thought. There are such things as mortal sins, and firing a hardworking man who is just trying to do his job is probably a big one!

Pat, however, was left with no choice. He returned to radio broadcasting at KABC Los Angeles. Until the scandals blew over, his face had to remain hidden.

But radio broadcasting didn't offer the high salary that TV did. The smaller paychecks weakened Pat's already tenuous grip on his fast-track lifestyle.

Pat's scream awakened Lois at 3:30 one morning. "What's wrong?" she cried in terror, fumbling for the light.

Pat was sitting upright in bed next to her. When he spoke, his voice trembled. "The devil... I saw him! He wants my soul!"

37

Surprise Decision

Fears of fluoride, anti-Semitism, and communism continued to loom over Elsinore. The optimism that formerly permeated the resort town seemed less and less likely ever to return. No one—not even those serving in the justice system—wanted to pour more trouble on a city that had already suffered such trauma. Five Riverside County Superior Court judges disqualified themselves from hearing the charges that had been leveled.

In addition to the desire to provide healing, those on the Superior Court were afraid to convict the unruly entourage of antagonists who were named in the indictment. The judges knew that many upstanding citizens had already become victims of character assassination by this group.

This turn of events gave an unexpected boost to Pat Michaels and other agitators who maintained that Elsinore's Jewish population had been targeted by state agencies.

Before long, the hearings were transferred to Indio, a small desert town off Route 10 between Palm Springs and the Mexican border. The trial, before Superior Court Judge Merrill Brown, was set for March 16, 1961. With one swift action, Brown suddenly dismissed the entire case. For the accused, this meant the nullification of all indictments.

Judge Brown remarked: "I am mindful of all the publicity Elsinore has received, and the quicker the litigation is brought to an end, the better for everyone."

Without doubt, Elsinore needed a break from its ongoing agony—no one argued with Judge Brown on that point. However, there was at least some speculation as to what (or who) truly influenced his decision. Was it sympathy? Or bribery? Some suspected George Chula of pulling the judge's strings. Chula had high-ranking friends in every county. Because of his questionable practices, he also had many foes in high places—some who couldn't wait to see him behind bars. Did Chula pay off the judge?

The Attorney General's office was quick to recommend an appeal to Judge Brown's decision. Elsinore's City Attorney Carl Kegley was the first one to face the appellate court. Would a small-town lawyer stand a chance against the renowned Attorney General Stanley Mosk?[5]

By this time, Mosk had made a name for himself in many high-profile cases. He was known as a civil rights champion, and it was he who had forced the Professional Golfers' Association of America to amend its bylaws to accept minority golfers. He later held the record on the California Supreme Court as the longest-serving Associate Justice.

Elsinore was Mosk's first case after he was elected to office, and he represented the State versus those who

---

[5] People v. Kegley 198 Cal. App. 2d 501 [Crim. No. 1590. Fourth Dist. Dec. 26, 1961]. Wikipedia.org / Stanley Mosk.

had muddied the state's waters. Accusations of anti-Semitism had caught Mosk's eye; as a Jew, advocacy for his people came naturally. In this instance though, he showed no partiality.

"Something is rotten in the state of Elsinore," Mosk said. His conscience would not allow a righteous cause to be reduced to an opportunistic exploit, even if it did help an oppressed minority. So he fought hard against the Elsinore agitators.

Carl Kegley had allegedly used his public office to embezzle city funds. The city clerk's testimony to the Grand Jury stated that Kegley indeed "sought payment to himself of certain amounts." According to the charges, Kegley claimed reimbursement for personal telephone use, for both toll-free calls and toll calls alike. Although his requests for payment might have raised some eyebrows in the City Treasurer's office, checks were cut nonetheless.

Kegley admitted that his calls were related to "personal private matters and not city business." An examination of the record disclosed more than fifty such calls, the majority of which were toll-free. Although these calls were personal and didn't cost a dime, Kegley requested handsome reimbursement for them. And in front of the AG he admitted what he'd done.

With his confession, however, Kegley argued that the Grand Jury had no probable cause for an indictment. His expert opinion was that the Jury failed to prove the intent to defraud. In his own defense, Kegley stated, "The false claims were an innocent mistake on my part." Favor weighing heavily on the side of the Grand Jury, Mosk sided with the Jury's evidence and against Kegley.

With the heat squarely focused on top city officials, other involved parties managed to escape prosecution and emerge unscathed. Charges against Pat Michaels and key agitators were ultimately put to rest, but there were plenty of remaining wounds to lick. The city, scarred by angry zealots, needed a healing. Dismissing the indictments certainly helped Elsinore in the long run, but did not serve the interest of "justice for all." Bitter feelings remained.

There was no good solution, but the judges and the Grand Jury did the best they could to balance justice and mercy… Justice for a few guilty parties, and mercy for the long-beleaguered city.

With charges dismissed, Pat Michaels felt a great weight lift from his shoulders. Still, when he closed his eyes at night, he saw demons.

38

Found Out

The scandal in Elsinore left a shadowy haze over Pat Michaels' life, one that he couldn't escape even in the safe haven of his broadcast booth. Callers continuously hounded him on the phone at his desk. His provocative reporting on the radio added to the media mayhem, causing phone lines to light up like fireworks on the Fourth of July. The attention didn't bother Pat. He was happy to take the calls, especially from those looking to wrangle. With his quick comebacks, he could cut callers down to size in moments.

Such lively conversations earned Pat a reputation among his coworkers. One colleague suggested he take calls on the air. This was a revolutionary idea; talk radio was unknown in the early 1960s. Eager to venture into new territory, KABC fully embraced the idea. Management agreed that a controversial personality was needed— someone listeners would "love to hate" and "hate to love." Pat was the ideal candidate.

With blessings from the boss, he was handed the perfect venue, and his polemical reputation promised success. As it turned out, Elsinore had evolved from a thorn in his side to a feather in his cap.

Not only had Pat escaped conviction for his involvement in the Elsinore scandal, he ultimately prospered from the ordeal. This boosted his confidence even further. He began taking greater risks, both occupationally and privately. Before long, the invincible radio legend was vacationing with his mistress.

"I'm off to cover a story in France for a couple of weeks," he announced to his hopelessly devoted wife. Pat spoke the truth but not the whole truth. He conveniently omitted one major detail—with whom he would be traveling! Lois only knew the invitation didn't extend to her.

Pat very well may have been covering a story, but he did a poor job of covering his tracks. During his absence, Lois received a phone call from an angry "business associate" to whom a considerable amount of money was owed. When she learned the nature of the business, Lois was in complete shock. It didn't seem possible that someone as outwardly pious as Pat could harbor secrets so dark. The caller, however, was very real, making threats and demanding pay.

"I know nothing about your business dealings with my husband!" Lois protested.

"You can't fool me!" a hostile voice fired back. "You're in this as deep as he is!"

"I have no part in this whatsoever!" Lois assured the caller.

"Baloney. You and Pat are tied together at the hip. Don't try to tell me you just pose for that magazine then punch out on a time clock or something."

"Do you have any idea who you are speaking to?"

Addressing Lois by the name of Pat's mistress sent red flags rocketing higher than Sputnik II. That's when she insisted on knowing the magazine's title. After the handset was returned to the cradle, Lois was off to the newsstand.

Never in her wildest dreams had Lois imagined buying pornography. With dark shades, a low-brimmed hat, and a high-collared coat, she found the courage. And she also found the publication she sought.

There on the magazine's front cover was the family boat, the *Bon Michelle*, with an unholy host of bare bodies frolicking on the upper deck. Front and center was Pat's secretary.

Not many days later, Lois received another devastating call, this time from a daycare facility. They too were demanding payment. Lois responded as before, "I know nothing about this." Once again, she was addressed by the name of Pat's mistress.

"It's for your child's care," the caller explained. "Your last check bounced."

Before the cradle could catch the receiver, Lois fell to the floor.

39

Winners and Losers

Not all of those implicated in the Elsinore scandal were indicted for their involvement. Those who caused the most trouble managed to escape the legal aftermath. Morris Kominsky, with his endless "sky is falling" tirades, gained notoriety, but that was about all the success he achieved. Most dismissed him as hyperparanoid, although not all agreed; his faithful comrades saw him as a champion for civil rights.

Indeed, Morris marched on the front lines to defend the oppressed. As noble as his efforts seemed, his doomsday disposition provided little relief for the downtrodden. Their cause did demand a voice, but Morris's credibility was increasingly tangled in a web of lies, leaving him powerless to effect positive change. And as for all the uproar Morris created in Elsinore, he walked away from the wreckage with barely a scratch.

In the end, most of the key members of the propaganda machine also escaped blame, leaving city officials to face all the charges. Elsinore's Mayor Thomas Bartlett and several other council members suffered the hardest blows. Ultimately, the Grand Jury held them responsible for violating a state mandate prohibiting the distribution of untreated spring water, and they also ascribed them blame for shutting off tap water against state orders.

Attorney General Stanley Mosk was again ready to prosecute. It was his last shot for an appeal, and his sense of justice prompted him to seek at least some retribution for the nasty deeds committed in Elsinore.

The Grand Jury transcript consisted of 960 pages and 67 exhibits, most of which focused on the *City of Hate* broadcast and related slander charges. Only one exhibit pertained to indictments against Bartlett and his fellow council members. Yet it was these public figures who were accused by the court.

According to the charges, they "feloniously and knowingly conspired to willfully and unlawfully violate the terms and provisions of a water permit issued by the State Department of Public Health of the State of California, said permit issued in accordance with the provisions of the Health and Safety Code."

The action further stated that city officials "caused 100 per cent mineral water to flow through the mains of the city of Elsinore in violation of the State Department of Health Water Permit."

As serious as the charges sounded, they were merely misdemeanors. Nevertheless, counsel fought hard for the defense. Weighing in their favor was the vague language written in a key piece of evidence.

The civic and state codes were purposely left open to interpretation as a convenience to those imposing them; thus finding proof that these violations had occurred was a challenge. The governing entities who created the codes failed to understand that, although the cryptic language met the government's ever-changing whims, most lawyers would find it easy to create a case stating either that "the law doesn't mean what it says" or "the law doesn't say what it means."

This is exactly the tack that the defense took, and a sparring match ensued between the prosecution and the defense, as each attempted to offer a proper interpretation of the codes in question. Because the language was unclear, so were the offenses.

Counsel for Thomas Bartlett charged that the Grand Jury not only failed to interpret the terms and provisions of the water permit correctly, but the jurors never even read the permit! According to the defense, they instead relied on the foggy memories and false interpretations of incompetent witnesses. Because of the Grand Jury's neglect in reviewing key evidence, a strong case was made that an uninformed and biased jury wrongfully indicted the defendants. This blunder created a major hurdle for the prosecution. Even had the language been clear on the permit, the fact remained that the charges were based solely on hearsay.

The case against all participants in the Elsinore matter simply fell apart.

40
Homeward Bound

What began as a typical day for Terrance ended in shock. Having finally escaped his second-grade classroom, he now focused on the steep climb to his cozy Sherman Oaks home on Del Gado Drive. His empty stomach made the ascent more agonizing than usual because his thermos had leaked lukewarm milk all over the inside of his Casper the Friendly Ghost lunchbox. When he'd opened the box at lunchtime, he found his baloney sandwich and graham crackers were sodden. Most of the meal Mom had packed was too unappetizing to eat.

The meager lunch of carrot sticks left Terrance feeling weak. He wasn't able to comprehend the big words in his *More Friends and Neighbors* reading book that afternoon. With head swimming and stomach growling, the child was in no mood for uphill hikes beneath the blazing sun. Yet this would be the least of his worries.

He had barely traveled two blocks from school when he heard his older brother calling in the distance.

"Terrance! Terrance!" Rick cried. "Where are you?"

"I'm over here!" Terrance called back. "Coming up the street! What do you want?"

When they found each other, Rick was not alone. With him was Mrs. Coffman who lived down the hill from the Michaels family. Her home had become a regular hangout for Terrance. Not only were Lois and Mrs. Coffman close friends, Terrance and Ed Coffman were classmates. The Coffman house also served as a convenient rest stop for Terrance when he was hiking home from school. There was always a plate full of buttery Lorna Doone cookies awaiting his arrival.

Sadly, the visit that spring day in 1964 had little to do with milk and cookies.

"You're coming home with me today," Mrs. Coffman announced. "You'll be spending the night." While Terrance always enjoyed goofing off with Ed, he instinctively sensed this wasn't a typical play date. Nor had he ever been an overnight guest before. "You and Rick will stay at least a couple of nights," Mrs. Coffman said. That was two nights too long.

"Why can't I go home?" Terrance asked with wide eyes.

Ever so gently, the dear lady explained the sad news. Del Gado Drive was no longer home. Dad was gone. A move was in the making.

Terrance had no words. No amount of Lorna Doone cookies could ease the pain.

Divorce was inevitable. Even Father Lawlor agreed. In fact, the priest insisted on it in these circumstances, despite his usually strict adherence to Catholic edicts about staying married. The facts spoke clearly however. Pat was juggling a second home with a second family. The church could never approve.

194

Pat pleaded with Lois not to divorce him, but she had no interest in sharing her husband with another wife. Pat's covert adult-entertainment business further sealed his fate. Everything Lois knew about her beloved husband had mutated into a cruel hoax that left a devastated home and a trail of broken hearts.

The 1960s were transitional for Pat—not just personally but also vocationally. He stopped pretending to be religious, stopped faking traditional values, and quit presenting hyperbole as factual news. That didn't mean his hyperbole wasn't profitable though. Pat understood that the world of talk radio wouldn't survive without an explosive mix of exaggeration and controversy.

As an early pioneer in the field, Pat mastered the art of shock-talk in the greater Los Angeles market. Using this platform he could be anything he wished, from far-left liberal to far-right conservative, as long as he provided raw emotion and drama.

There was no shortage of drama on KABC's *Pat Michaels Show*. With it also came frequent recruiting calls from other major-market stations. Because of his love of the sea, the offer from KNEW in San Diego appealed most to Pat. The salty air brought fresh ideas. And he found himself with more time to work now that Lois and the kids were out of the picture.

It was on KNEW that the *I Hate Pat Michaels* show was born. His unique brand of radio took off like wildfire. Callers flooded the lines to argue hot topics, only to be berated and chopped into pieces by Pat. Milking the hostility for all it was worth, KNEW saturated the San

Diego area with billboards and bumper stickers boldly declaring "I Hate Pat Michaels."

The ad campaign didn't win him scores of friends, but his show scored high ratings. The promise of further success beckoned from all horizons. As for Elsinore, she faded from his rearview mirror like taillights on a passing car.

Terrance cried himself to sleep every night for a year.

41

Dream Extreme

Tensions finally began to calm in Elsinore. The legal and media spotlights had faded, and most people made an effort to forget all they'd been through. Some neighbors, who previously were antagonists, now shook hands over backyard fences.

Even so, the lake levels were low, which meant that people who had deserted their once-beloved resort still weren't interested in returning. The populace at large had come to think of Elsinore as a dustbowl. Tourists, home investors, and entrepreneurs stayed away, and commerce continued to languish. As a result, economic recovery in Elsinore seemed an impossible dream.

Governor Pat Brown ultimately came to the rescue. He negotiated with leaders in Arizona and Nevada to pipe in some of their surplus water from the Colorado River.

Plans for revitalizing Elsinore took shape. A canal was constructed, and in February 1964 the impossible became possible. Roaring white rapids from the east flooded into Elsinore, restoring the massive lake back to its former glory. Brimming now at 1240 feet above sea level, stigmas left by the *City of Hate* were washed away, replaced by fanciful tales of sea serpents that just might return from their lairs to the depths beneath the new young skiers skimming above them.

The refilling of Southern California's largest natural lake was met with widespread enthusiasm. No longer would Elsinore be remembered for its troubled past; a bright future awaited her. Swimmers, sunbathers, power boaters, and fishermen raced to her fresh waters. On their heels came eager homebuyers and businessmen with money. Elsinore was not only recovering, she was surging to an even greater heights as a recreational hot spot. Tumbleweeds disappeared, and colorful welcome mats replaced tattered "closed" signs.

Elsinore's revival ushered in an improvement in local leadership. Thomas Yarborough, who had had the misfortune of sitting on city counsel during the fluoride scandal, now earned well-deserved respect and favor from the community. In 1966 he was sworn into office as mayor, becoming the first African American in California's history ever to hold such a post.

Yarborough not only restored integrity to the mayor's seat, he also brought new heart, spirit, and vision to a town that desperately needed a makeover. Thanks in great degree to Yarborough's influence, Elsinore was no longer a forlorn wasteland. She was back on the map.

Yarborough's term was tragically cut short. He died in an auto accident during his final year in office, but his legacy lives on. A park in downtown Elsinore bears his name. The property was donated to the city by Yarborough himself, and today it serves as tribute to a man, who arrived in Elsinore as a humble handyman, and who offered his service to a community that gave him a chance.

In 1972 the town council proposed a name change to rejuvenate tourism further. By popular decision, "City of Elsinore" was renamed "Lake Elsinore." The rebranding stimulated more interest in the locale, and vacationers brought campers and tents to enjoy nature in renovated campgrounds.

Some challenges still remained for Lake Elsinore; in 1981 the ferocious El Niño trade winds brought the worst flooding in Lake Elsinore's history. The storms destroyed many homes and businesses. With power sources submerged, rebuilding in key areas was impossible for several years.

Thanks to federal grants, the city rose again. With a costly overhaul and creative marketing, additional multitudes decided they'd like to "Dream Extreme in Lake Elsinore." By 2007 Lake Elsinore was recognized as California's fastest-growing city.

In Lake Elsinore today, almost all those who remember the *City of Hate* scandals have drifted away like thistledown on the wind.

42

Rise and Fall

Thomas Yarborough wasn't the only person to achieve notoriety after the Elsinore scandal. Attorney General Stanley Mosk continued climbing higher on the legislative ladder. Although justice never swung in Mosk's favor regarding the Elsinore case, a top seat awaited him at the State Capitol. Governor Pat Brown appointed him to the California Supreme Court in September 1964. As California's longest-serving justice on record, he is credited with numerous landmark decisions.

Mosk ruled against racial quotas for college admissions, and he also voted in favor of laws requiring parental consent for minors seeking abortions. As a professed champion of the people, Mosk was noted for developing the constitutional doctrine of "independent state grounds," which deemed that "individual rights are not dependent solely on interpretation of the U.S. Constitution by the U.S. Supreme Court and other federal courts, but also can be found in state constitutions."

Stanley Mosk served until his death in 2001, having become the most influential justice in California history.

As an accomplished freelance writer, Morris Kominsky used his "red pen" to expose efforts of the U.S. government to quell the spread of fascism and communism in America. His life's work included the publication of one alarming conspiracy theory after another. A major achievement was his lengthy book entitled *The Hoaxers: Plain Liars, Fancy Liars and Damned Liars*. The tome's intended objective was spelled out in its preface—to offer a well-researched "study of the trends in the United States of America towards Fascism and a Third World War."

Morris also promised to publish a second volume called *America Faces Disaster*, which was to continue exposing "the story of the groups, individuals, and policies that endanger the citizens of the USA, as well as the rest of mankind." For unknown reasons, this second volume never materialized.

Other collections of Kominsky's work are preserved in the Southern California Library for Social Studies and Research in Los Angeles, as well as in the American Jewish Archives in New York City. Morris Kominsky was laid to rest in April 1975.

George Chula leaves behind a colorful legacy. Convinced he was the best defense lawyer money could buy, Chula was hired by the notorious Brotherhood of Eternal Love. Members of this radical cult believed that tripping-out on hallucinogenic drugs was a religious experience, and they hoped to start a "psychedelic revolution" in the United States.

By this time Dr. Timothy Leary was also forming his own brand of religion among the youth counterculture.

With his message of "tune in, turn on, drop out," LSD became the new sacrament of the hippie movement. Leary's message earned him high honor among members of the Brotherhood of Eternal Love.

The Brotherhood grew to be one of the largest manufacturers of LSD in the nation. As business increased, their hashish and cocaine trade expanded to countries in the Middle East. With these vast operations, Federal agents soon described the Brotherhood as a "hippie mafia," and the Feds increasingly suspected that Chula was an informant for the hippies. Whether or not this was true, Chula maintained friends in high places, both in the Brotherhood and in the government. If traffickers ever fell prey to a drug bust, Chula knew how to make the charges disappear.

By this time, Leary was a high-profile cult icon, and it was impossible for Chula, or anyone else, to make Leary's charges evaporate when he was arrested. Found guilty of drug possession, Leary was sentenced to prison. The Brotherhood was not pleased, and they immediately coughed up $30,000 to break their guru out of jail. For months, Leary remained at large while federal agents pursued him. He was finally apprehended in Afghanistan and was brought back to the United States in chains.

In an unusual turn of events, Leary cooperated with Feds in their quest to capture Chula. Leary claimed that Chula had supplied him with hashish during his in time in prison. Although Leary's admission earned him some points with authorities, it was Leary's girlfriend Joanna who ultimately took Chula down.

In a sting operation, with federal agents wiretapping from an adjacent room, Joanna lured Chula to a motel where she seduced him and purchased cocaine from him. After his arrest, Chula found himself behind bars, and Leary was released after testifying against him.

After helping Pat Michaels with the Elsinore case, Attorney George Chula had envisioned his name in lights. Now he was known as Booking Number 00-543-23 in Module C-17.

Obituary

In bold print, the *Orange County Register* announced: "Pat Michaels, Longtime Local Reporter, Dies at 84." The date was August 27, 2010.

Flaws aside, Pat is best remembered for his achievements as a reporter. Jeff Overley wrote the obituary:

> Pat Michaels, who spent a career covering Southern California news for television, radio, and newspapers and became well known for both chronicling and becoming immersed in Newport Beach's social scene, has died. He was 84.
>
> Michaels, who died Monday in Rancho Mirage, hosted the public television show *Your Newport Today* and wrote a column for Register community newspapers covering Newport Beach for more than a decade.
>
> Despite battling lung cancer and other ailments in recent years, he continued producing a weekly digest of neighborhood news and over-the-fence chatter until just a few weeks ago.
>
> "I think he would want to be remembered as a professional journalist—he never stopped being it, just never," said Paula Michaels, his wife of 50 years.

Patrick Francis Michaels was born November 5, 1925, in Superior, Wisconsin, one of three children. His father, a newspaper reporter, contracted tuberculosis and died in confinement when Michaels was young. His mother, left to provide for the family, placed her son in foster homes and an orphanage for many of his early years.

She moved the kids to Orange County in the mid-1930s, and when Pat was about 10, she gave him a small printer he used to create his own newspaper, a passion that never left him.

"He lived, breathed and just slept it," Paula Michaels said. "He really loved it."

At 16, Michaels ran away from home and joined the Marine Corps, serving in combat at Guadalcanal. Upon returning home, he found a job covering World War II for New York's Mutual Broadcasting System. At 18, he was among the youngest network correspondents.

Back in California, later positions would find him conducting investigations for KTLA and managing KWIZ-FM. He developed his own style, finding news by embedding himself in local culture, evidenced by his joining of the Balboa Bay Club in 1956.

"It was the place where I could hang out to get all kinds of stories," Michaels said in a 1994 interview. "There were always movie stars and politicians. ... It was the place where all of Orange

County went to have its charity events, its political fund-raisers."

Michaels also made an unsuccessful City Council bid in 1986, declaring he would "bring a reporter's training for uncovering facts into government and use my businessman's skills to resolve problems.

"I love Newport Beach and will conscientiously serve it and its citizens," he said at the time.

In his media role, Michaels long ago began dishing the sort of "hyper-local" tidbits—quick profiles, amusing neighborhood mishaps—that have lately come into vogue as newspapers try to shore up their relevance. He was especially known for printing corny quotes from casual conversations.

One example: "Katie Keating, at a Costa Mesa bridal shop: 'I used to wonder why women did so much crying at weddings, and then I took a look at some of the grooms.'"

Another: "Server at The Ritz to Jack Palmer: 'Our soup is only made from the finest and freshest du jours available.'"

Paul Danison, Register editor for Newport Beach, described Michaels as "part historian, part humorist, and the consummate community journalist."

"He was a friendly guy who couldn't make it a city block without stopping to chat with someone," Danison said. "He was well-respected, an engaging and entertaining writer, and he reflected the community in his weekly columns."

Michaels moved to Palm Springs about a decade ago and split his time between the desert and Newport Beach, but preserved strong ties with civic groups such as the Newport Harbor American Legion and the Rotary Club of Newport-Balboa.

"He was always warm and caring," said Dave Rudder of the Newport Harbor Elks Lodge. "He was truly interested in making Orange County, and certainly the world, a better place. He just had a heart for people."

Eulogy

Despite the claim that Pat had a heart for people and wanted to make the world a better place, only a few came to pay their respects to the deceased reporter—mostly just family and a handful of others. As he was put to rest, the military offered a well-deserved war hero's salute at Pat's graveside. The bugle played, shots were fired, and a flag was placed on his coffin.

As for me, Terrance Michaels, the youngest of four children from Pat's first marriage, I was granted the privilege of offering the following words:

I'm not here today as a pastor, nor did I come to preach. I'm here for the same reason as everyone else—to honor a man I love. I'm here today as my father's son.

Some relationships aren't easy to describe. A popular answer might be, "it's complicated." I prefer to say, "it's simple." That's not to say family never gets complicated. Kids grow up. There's marriage and sometimes remarriage. Life gets hectic. People relocate. Sometimes it's the kids; other times it's the parents. Circumstances change. People change. Family dynamics change. There are always complications or challenges when it comes to family ties. But I'm not one to focus on complicated issues. I enjoy life a lot more when I focus on the simple.

The simple fact is that Pat Michaels was my father. The simple fact is that his blood courses through my veins. The simple fact is that I would not exist if it were not for him. The simple fact is that love isn't complicated. Love rises above the complications. Love hopes all things, believes all things, and endures all things. Love never fails. Love keeps no record of wrongs.

The memories I choose to hold of my father are all fond ones: From my earliest memories of watching scary movies in black and white, while he fed me chocolate-covered malt balls, to my most recent memory of being at his hospital bedside where I fed him morsels of water from a small sponge.

I remember Dad in the studio of KGO in San Francisco, watching him do his show. I was always proud of his accomplishments in radio and TV. I still remember the Marine's Hymn to this day. He taught it to me. I remember his war stories, his medals, and his uniform. I remember Christmases, trips to Catalina, and Dad teaching me sail. I remember the first bike he bought me, and my first fishing pole. I'll always remember the words he spoke to me when I last saw him. "I'm proud of you son."

You see, love doesn't have to be complicated. The complications in life will spoil love if you let them. I suppose this is why I keep clear of religion. As for me, religion gets far too complicated. It muddles things up. It can distract you from what's truly important. The simple fact is—God is love. He loves us and He desires to be loved by us. God demonstrated His love for us at the cross of Calvary. He sent his Son to die for our sins. He offers forgiveness with the promise of heaven.

That is the hope I have. One day I will join my dad in heaven. I wish I could have spent more time with him in the here and now. I wish the miles had not separated us. But I have all eternity to look forward to. I will catch up with dad on the other side. Until then, I will hold onto those precious moments we shared.

Final Thoughts

I inherited my love of writing from my father. Although he wasn't around to fan my creative flames, he did provide the genepool. I credit my mother for encouraging me. Dad never knew of my abilities or my desires. Time and distance kept us apart—along with a lack of interest on his part and resentment on mine.

In my earlier years I sought to win my father's approval by following his footsteps; I pursued a career in radio, but this path didn't fit my personality. I had neither the passion nor the confidence required of an on-air personality.

Despite my shortcomings, I graduated from broadcasting school and easily landed several disc-jockey jobs. Soon I found myself working for my father at a station in San Bernardino—not far from Elsinore. Working for my dad didn't help our relationship. We were opposites: He was still pursuing worldly success, and by that time I was more interested in denying myself, taking up my cross, and following Christ (Luke 9:23).

Working with Dad proved not only painful but also eventually impossible. My father cut me loose. I realized then that broadcasting wasn't for me... plus it wasn't the bridge between the two of us that I'd hoped.

A passion for God eventually led me into full-time ministry. I at last found purpose and fulfillment by following Christ's footsteps. I learned that God's affection isn't won through performance or ritual. His love just exists (Exodus 3:14), and this unconditional love erased my ache of bitterness and replaced it with gentle forgiveness.

I never did grow close to my dad. Thanks to my relationship with Christ though, the burden of winning Dad's affection was lifted and my resentment evaporated. Forgiveness from God was the cure I needed.

I'm now completely devoted to serving God and His people. And I consider writing as a gift that must be received and exercised faithfully and creatively.

Elsinore: The City of Hate Conspiracy is my fifth book. My earlier works are devotional or inspirational in nature, so this work of historical fiction is a departure. To make the story more accessible, I have added some scenes and dialogue, but the main facts of the Elsinore story are true and are gleaned from my research.

The lessons of Elsinore are many. The shattered Ten Commandments above the door to the synagogue remind us that we are all sinners and lawbreakers. No one comes to the Father except through faith in the sacrifice of God's Son Jesus Christ (Romans 3:23; Romans 6:23).

Hatred, resentment, anger, bitterness can never be conquered by more of the same. Although no one could control the drought in Elsinore, people made willful choices to lie and slander about the circumstances.

God reminds us that only the blood of Jesus can cleanse our unclean, law-breaking hearts. We have a

212

choice to trust Jesus, but until we make that choice, we are slaves to sin.

We can find forgiveness by faith in His sinless sacrifice and, thus, our lives can be filled to overflowing with the Holy Spirit, just as the waters finally flooded back into Lake Elsinore.

Hate yields death and destruction. Only love sets us free.

"Love suffers long and is kind; love does not envy; love does not parade itself, is not puffed up; does not behave rudely, does not seek its own, is not provoked, thinks no evil; does not rejoice in iniquity, but rejoices in the truth; bears all things, believes all things, hopes all things, endures all things. Love never fails." (1 Corinthians 13:4–8a)

Do not resist the open arms of God. It's your choice. Our Heavenly Father loves even those who refuse love. He proved it on the Cross and saves those who believe.

For more information about the love and forgiveness of Jesus, go to:

http://www.harvest.org/knowgod/

We're praying for you!

Made in the USA
Columbia, SC
04 July 2018